Praise for R. G. Alexander's *Midnight Falls*

"Midnight Falls is the fourth book in the Children of the Goddess series and once again, I am impressed with R. G. Alexander's storytelling ability."

~ *Literary Nymphs*

Look for these titles by
R. G. Alexander

Now Available:

Children of the Goddess Series
Regina in the Sun (Book 1)
Lux in Shadow (Book 2)
Twilight Guardian (Book 3)
Midnight Falls (Book 4)

Not in Kansas
Surrender Dorothy

Three for Me?

Shifting Reality Series
My Shifter Showmance

Wicked Series
Wicked Sexy

Wasteland Series
The Priestess

Midnight Falls

R. G. Alexander

A Samhain Publishing, Ltd. publication.

Samhain Publishing, Ltd.
577 Mulberry Street, Suite 1520
Macon, GA 31201
www.samhainpublishing.com

Midnight Falls
Copyright © 2010 by R. G. Alexander
Print ISBN: 978-1-60504-792-8
Digital ISBN: 978-1-60504-805-5

Editing by Bethany Morgan
Cover by Anne Cain

This book is a work of fiction. The names, characters, places, and incidents are products of the writer's imagination or have been used fictitiously and are not to be construed as real. Any resemblance to persons, living or dead, actual events, locale or organizations is entirely coincidental.

All Rights Are Reserved. No part of this book may be used or reproduced in any manner whatsoever without written permission, except in the case of brief quotations embodied in critical articles and reviews.

First Samhain Publishing, Ltd. electronic publication: October 2009
First Samhain Publishing, Ltd. print publication: August 2010

Dedication

For Cookie–Love is the reason. And to Beth and my Smutketeers: Lilli Feisty, Crystal Jordan and the glorious Eden Bradley, for always being there. I would also like to acknowledge the readers who have told me that they have fallen just as in love with these characters as I did when Regina first started to dance beside me and begged me to write her story. Thank you.

Chapter One

"Help me! Oh, God, somebody please help me!"

He covered his ears at the grating, alien intrusion. Wild boars mating held nothing on that sound. *Have to find it. Have to stop it.* He stepped off the high limb of the tree where he'd taken his rest for the night, falling straight down to land, crouched, at its base.

"Help!"

He ran toward the noise, the mountainside forest a blur as he raced to the source of the unwanted intrusion. His nostrils flared. Woman. Human. She was doused with a repellent, an oily citrus that made him want to gag. Another odor, this one more familiar, covered that stink with its own. A dark smile lifted his lips, and he increased his speed.

Shadow.

Again? They'd left him alone for decades, why were they bothering him now? A hot poker of pain in his temples made him swear, freezing only moments before he reached the clearing where the screams had originated. Never mind. He didn't care why. He could never have too much of a good thing. There was nothing better to break up the monotony than playing with paranoid dogs.

"Silence her, she did her job. His scent is close. Now I will succeed and make the others look like fools." The voice was nervous, merely pretending confidence. Not an Alpha then. Pity. Anything less than an Alpha tasted sour.

"I still don't understand why we have to kill it. Gyvain was very specific that it was to be left alone. Why are we listening to that a—"

"Gyvain is dead. And he was never *my* Alpha, nor yours. It is an affront to the memory of our fallen fathers to leave that abomination alive. They say he looks exactly like the Storm Bringer. Unfortunately Gyvain's son and his followers let the family have that body to burn. I think I'll take this one's head as a trophy, so that every one who sees it knows what I have done."

The names were like shards of glass rammed into his ears, and the throbbing in his head increased. Luckily, a feminine whimper distracted them from their conversation. The second Shadow murmured soothingly to the frightened girl. "Why should I care about things that happened before my time when I have such a gorgeous creature in my arms? Isn't she a pretty thing? I didn't know this side of the world had such pretty things. If we get him can I still have *her*? Keep her as you said after we slay the animal?"

Cocky youth. Calling *him* an animal? The insult more than the threat to the terrorized woman sent fog rolling in around the two Shadow Wolves and their captive.

His fog.

He knew they could smell him, that the fog was only a momentary confusion, meant to terrorize and distract more than protect him. But that was what he wanted. So few things gave him pleasure, but it gave him pleasure to scare them. And they were scared. They had come onto his territory, had come for him, and again and again they underestimated his abilities. Abilities that only seemed to grow stronger with time.

One leaping stride had him directly behind the nervous one, who was too busy growling to notice he had a visitor. He sank his fangs deep, one hand over the villain's mouth to keep him quiet as he drank the dark blood. Just as he'd thought. Sour. The images the blood brought did nothing to ease his pain. But it gave him the sustenance he needed. Satisfied him in a way the local wildlife never could. He lifted his mouth, smiling as the slender neck twisted easily in his hands, breaking with a satisfying crunch.

The cocky Were called out to his now silent companion, but it was too late. The woman had fallen free to the hard ground, and he was flailing in the air, his claws desperate to pry the large, strong hand from his throat.

The lovely dark skinned girl looked at her savior, squinting through the mist. "Thank you. Thank you, you saved my—"

"Run."

He wanted to drink her dry, to drain her blood. He knew instinctively that it would be sweet, would erase the bitter taste of Shadow on his tongue. Where were her instincts? Humans lacked all sense of self-preservation.

"Run now."

She backed away at his growl, tripping over her shredded backpack. Her richly scented blood poured down her knees, tempting him as she scrambled into the woods. She didn't look back. So. Not that stupid after all.

"You may as well kill me." The gasping Were in his grip continued to struggle. "I won't tell you where the others are. Won't tell you who you—"

Snap.

Silence. Blessed silence. He turned and slowly walked back the way he had come. He could have told the bastard he didn't want to know, that he didn't care. But it would have been a lie.

Still, after all these years, he knew better.

Curiosity may not kill the cat, but it sure as hell gave him one hell of a headache.

Three years. It was less than a moment to a vampire who counted time in centuries. But so much had happened since Liz had been gone this time. Good things. And horrible things. She watched a raven fly overhead and smiled. "Does the Mediator know you're out here?"

The bird's image shimmered, transforming into an exotic female with dusky skin and golden eyes. The white streaks in her long, dark hair only enhanced her youthful sensuality. They were badges of honor from what she'd suffered at the hands of Grey Wolf. "You've gotten very good at that, Regina."

"I still wish I could change into something more intimidating. I'm glad you're here, Liz. I think you need to know what to expect before you go inside. And Zander always knows where I am. So does Max." Regina rolled her almond shaped eyes, but Liz could see she was relieved a Sariel guard was nearby. Everyone had been thrown by the recent attacks.

"So Max is watching over you since Kit got married?" Regina's hand slid through Liz's arm, squeezing gently. Did Regina think she needed comfort? Kit had been her lover, for a time, but they'd both known it was temporary. She was truly happy for him.

"Kit and Jesse were visiting her brother in America. The last time he called, it sounded like he was a little overwhelmed by his new in-laws. Zander said Kit had been trained for battle, but didn't have a clue how to deal with family game night."

Liz smirked. Jesse and her brother had lived their lives believing they were only human. They'd only found out a few years ago that her mother had been in love with a god. One of the Mother's children. To live normally after that had to be difficult. "Jesse's father hasn't been able to help with our current situation then? You'd think blood counted for something."

"He can't interfere anymore. The last time was a special situation, I told you. His brother Ba'al was involved."

"Two gods, scorpion men, a wedding. I miss all the excitement. And I heard through the grapevine that the Weres, Truebloods and Unborns are soon to sign a treaty."

"It's true. And it's been a real coup for Zander. Trade and information sharing, even ambassadors from each species. In fact, Zander is trying to lay the groundwork to add Kit's people, the Igigi, to the treaty. The giants are a private people, and they aren't technically the children of the Goddess, but now that Ba'al's sacrifice is no longer hanging over their heads, they are more open to outsiders. Of course, that's on hold..."

It was disturbing, the merging between their worlds. It was happening faster than she'd ever imagined. Political and personal alliances were being made. Peacefully. Smoothly. Times were changing. It was hard for Liz to take in. To believe. "When I first met you, Reggie, my little Gypsy, I knew the laws against changing a Reader. You were such a forlorn little thing. And the men in your family." She sneered. "That father of yours was actually planning to sell you to some dirty merchant. You deserved better. I think I saw myself in you." She shook her head, looking at the star filled night sky. "But I didn't know that night would bring this to pass. That you would be Zander Sariel's *grathita*. That a man from the purest line of Truebloods would ever find his mate in an Unborn, let alone one with your abilities. I don't think I really believed in the Mother's Message."

But Mal had. Her late husband Malcolm Abaddon had believed in The Mother, the creator of Trueblood, Were and

Human species alike. Unlike Liz, he'd believed that the werewolves and vampires had been created to watch over the world of fragile humans. Destiny, not genetics. He also believed in the Mother's Message, the prophecy of the Goddess said a Reader would turn all the old rules upside down. Change everything. He'd been right about that. He'd been right about a lot of things. She could only hope she'd done right by *him*, and that wherever he was, she hadn't shamed him by creating the Deva Clan.

Liz hesitated outside the Abaddon home. "Tell me, Reggie. Why are we here? I can't believe Nicolette, of all people... I told her what this family had done to Malcolm, their precious son. You know Sebastian joined forces with that Shadow Grey Wolf and had him murdered. His own brother."

Would the crime have been possible if he'd been within the safety of Abaddon land? If he hadn't married an Unborn? It was one of the questions that haunted her. That kept her fighting for her dead husband's cause.

For some unknown reason, Nicolette had come to stay here at Abaddon manor. Nicolette had been the one who had remained at her side during her darkest days, after she'd left this place. She knew about the Abaddons, about the Trueblood's prejudice. It was Nicolette who had helped her put her plan to create a clan for the vampire outcasts in motion.

Unborns, like they were, were for the most part accidents made by libidinous Truebloods searching for their true blood mates. Many were killed when they didn't experience Unity, but some escaped. Some survived. Liz had been an exception, created and kept in love. But when she realized how heartless the clans and their elders could be, realized the danger Nicolette and others constantly faced, alone and unprotected, the Deva Clan was born.

The Abaddons weren't to be trusted. Not even the mad, old Elder, who'd been taken off the council after the truth about Sebastian and Grey Wolf had come out, thanks to Regina.

Regina sighed, drawing Liz out of her musings. "I don't know why she came here. She's visited other clans before this, had her affairs, but I knew this was different. When Elder Abaddon invited her to stay with him and she accepted, she asked me not to pry, not to use my abilities to read her. I had to respect her wishes. You should know these last few years Nicolette has shined. She's been totally in her element as the Deva representative. I know you think this is your fault for not accepting a seat at the table, but if you'd seen the way she had the Elders wrapped around her finger, you would know you made the right decision."

A familiar voice came out of the darkness. "Did you tell her, Reggie?"

"Tell me what, Lux? That your being out here instead of at Nicolette's side means your amazing skills as a Healer have failed? Is she gone?"

Liz watched Lux drag a frustrated hand through his striking burgundy hair as he came closer. She had always thought him handsome. But his loyalty to Malcolm, his friendship and help after her husband had been slain, meant more to her than any temporary intimacy they could have had.

Not that she would stand a chance now anyway. Lux had claimed his *grathitas*. The only Trueblood in history to have two as far as she knew. Weres no less. The new Alpha of the uniting Were packs and a female with more power than any one being should have. Arygon and Sylvain. Liz had reasons to dislike the pair of them, but they'd made Lux happier than he'd ever been, and neither one of them could help their connection with Grey Wolf. Thank the Mother that shaman was dead. She was only sorry she hadn't been the one to kill him.

She noticed Regina and Lux share a speaking glance, and he sighed. "She isn't dead, Liz. But, she isn't responsive either. Priestess Magriel and Reggie have both tried to reach her telepathically, but her mind is a void. It's like she went somewhere else and left her body behind."

Liz bit the inside of her cheek until she tasted blood. "What happened?"

He shook his head, his gaze shifting away from hers guiltily. "We don't know."

"Bullshit." She gripped his shirt and dragged him closer, her upper lip curling to reveal her fangs. Lux snarled back and the air crackled with electricity. "Fuck all, Lizzy, *this* is why we didn't want you to come yet. Regina should have waited until we knew more."

"She deserves to know what's going on, Lux."

Liz knew her smile was less than comforting. "Yes, *she* does. Tell me."

Lux pried her fingers off his shirt and gripped her hands in his own. "We're not sure. Elder Abaddon's blood servant said he saw Nicolette meeting someone outside the manor gates. It wasn't the first time. But that night something happened. They were ambushed, attacked. By the time the servant arrived at the gate, they'd disappeared. Nicolette was found unconscious near the standing stones on Abaddon land. But...the man she was meeting was nowhere to be found."

Liz looked over at Regina, who sent her an image that made her growl, her eyes starting to glow. "Jasyn Dydarren? She was meeting with Arygon's brother? *He's* responsible?"

An angry female voice made the trio turn in surprise. "No! Damn you, Liz, don't you dare blame Jasyn for this. He was taken trying to *protect* her."

Shit. She hadn't realized Hannah was here. Nicolette had made the elfin blonde a part of their Unborn family in the nineteen twenties, when a car accident had left her near death. "Protect her? After a lifetime of vocal hatred? You expect me to believe that Jasyn Dydarren actually fought to protect the woman who'd slept with his father, revealed Arygon's sexuality to his pack and transformed you into the thing he most hated? The Jasyn I know could barely stand to be in the same room with her. Don't let your feelings for the Beta blind you, lass."

"It's true, Liz." Lux tightened his hands on hers, his look quelling. "Jasyn changed after his stay with the Igigi. He seemed...lighter somehow. More sure of himself." His gaze landed meaningfully on Hannah. "Sure of what he wanted. Besides, the servant saw him fighting off the beasts, until he was overcome and taken away."

Liz studied Hannah's tear stained face and lowered her chin in acknowledgement, feeling like she'd just kicked a puppy. "I'll withhold judgment. You said beasts. Weres then?"

Hannah nodded. "From what Sylvain sensed and the mark burned into Nicolette's temple, it looks like Shadow Wolves."

They marked her? Someone was going to pay. "We've killed Grey Wolf and his father Gyvain. Hell, we have the *Antara* and a Reader, two women they know could destroy every last one of them. What are there, like ten of them left? Why would they be so bold? And what could those black magic bastards possibly want with Jasyn?"

"We aren't sure, but Elder Abaddon is babbling that his son is coming back from the grave for revenge." Liz pulled away from Lux and turned to face her older brother Zander. They had her surrounded now, trying to calm her before she did something rash, she was sure.

The blond, broad shouldered Mediator of the Clan Trust

held Regina close in the crook of his arm, his face grim. "Sadly, I do not believe we'll get anything more coherent than that from him. As twisted as he has always been, no man should outlive his children. And he has lost all of his to violent ends. And now...Nicolette."

Liz began to pace, she felt caged. She needed to go up and see Nicolette, she needed to tear her attackers limb from limb. But first, she needed answers. "Goddess knows I've rarely understood Nicolette's taste in men, but Malcolm's *father*? That bitter nutcase? What was she thinking?"

Regina bit her lip. "I told you I didn't pry, not even with Jasyn. He said he needed some time away from Dydarren land, and I took him at his word." She glanced up at her husband. "I hesitate to mention it, because he is so young, but I don't think he has the same control I do. He may know some—"

"No. Don't start that again, my *priya*. Alexei is only six years old."

"What? What does your son have to do with this?"

Lux lowered his voice, leaning closer to Liz as Regina and her blood mate stared each other down, communicating silently. "You know what he was like as a toddler? Well his abilities have only grown since then. We knew he would be special, the child of a Reader and a Mediator from the purest bloodline, how could he not be? But there seems to be no end to his talents. Things that take other Truebloods hundreds of years to master, he does with ease. And his mother's ability to read and manipulate the thoughts of others seems even stronger in him. A fact which often gets my precocious nephew into serious trouble with his father."

Zander crossed his arms, controlled rage clenching his jaw. "My son doesn't need to be exposed to this."

"He already is, you stubborn ass." Regina put her hands on

her hips, defiant beside her towering husband. "He hasn't spoken for days, not since he told us where to find her. He may know something and just be too afraid to tell us."

"Jesse's father can't help us, and he's a damn god. What makes you think Alexei can?"

Hannah spoke up, looking desperate. "Nicolette loves Alexei, she spoils him rotten. You told me yourself that he always knew when she was coming. What mood she was in. Maybe he sensed something before she closed off. Maybe she told him what happened to her. To...to Jasyn."

Zander sighed, but refused to waver. "I can't bend on this. I won't allow him to come here...but, after we've seen Nicolette, Regina and I will speak to him."

Liz kept her mouth shut, but her own thoughts were more in line with the Mediator's. Why put a child through this? Even one as extraordinary as Alexei? "I want to see her."

"Are you going to be okay, Liz?"

She smiled, in truth this time, at Lux. He was a good friend to worry. Was she going to be okay walking into a home she'd been forbidden to enter for so long, seeing a man who had cursed her and threatened to disown Malcolm for refusing to kill her after his bite made her an Unborn instead of his *grathita*?

"I'm not the insecure, backward lass I once was. The real question is, will *he* be okay? Especially if I find he had anything to do with this." Goddess, she hoped he had.

The house was exactly as she remembered it. Ostentatious and frighteningly ornate. A vampire's Graceland. The fact that a wonderful man like Malcolm had been raised here was baffling. But he himself had told her that the Sariels had been the family of his heart, the Abaddons merely blood relations that he was forced to acknowledge.

Horrific statues lined the hallway, and elaborate frescos of fanged angels gorged themselves overhead. She felt nauseous. Nicolette had, during her years as a Venetian courtesan, been surrounded by some of the most exquisite artwork the world had to offer. Why would she choose to live in this gallery of the grotesque?

Her gaze strayed down the hall toward the Great Room where she knew one special painting was hung as the others guided her up the stairs. She'd been in awe of Malcolm when she'd first seen it, but he would have none of her admiration. He was no hero, he'd told her. Merely a soldier in a war that had to be waged. A hollow victory, he often called it. And he a paper hero.

That painting displayed why, though Mal's family had attacked him privately, they dared not push him too far in public. It depicted a pivotal battle during the Great War. The war between the Truebloods and Shadow Wolves fought hundreds of years ago. A battle that would never have been won without Malcolm Abaddon. He was a legend. A hero, no matter what he had said to the contrary. A fact his family had used for their own selfish ends again and again.

"She's in here, Liz. They told us Nicolette specifically requested this room." Liz nodded absently. She couldn't blame her. This *was* the nicest part of the house. Malcolm's suite. They'd spent three days here after he'd first changed her before they were "asked" to leave.

It was a large suite, two bedrooms connected by a spacious, if sterile, living room. Somehow the empty bedroom had always made her sad for Malcolm. Sebastian had had his twin, Sari, to play with. Tell secrets to. The two had been united, both in their poor life choices and their dislike of their elder brother. In the end, manipulated by Grey Wolf, Sebastian and Sari had even shared their tragic deaths. But Malcolm had never even had the comfort of a close sibling in this cold home.

She bit the inside of her cheek again, this time to hold back a self-mocking sound. She'd left three years ago to finally let go of these memories, to leave the past in the past, and the dead buried. Now here she was, right back where she'd started. Hip deep in memories. Only now, she could lose someone else. Nicolette.

Regina slid her hand into Liz's, and she squeezed gratefully. As a rule she would rather have her heart ripped from her chest than show any sign of weakness, but Reggie no doubt knew what she was feeling anyway, and she appreciated the support. Especially when they walked through the living room, seemingly untouched after all these years, and into the extra bedroom that she'd never had the chance to explore.

The only people in the room were the old tattooed priestess, Glynn Magriel, and a tall, spindly man who was obviously Elder Abaddon's blood servant. They never lasted long, and this one looked to be on his last legs.

Nicolette lay still as death on the bed, her chest barely moving, heartbeat terrifyingly slow to her untrained ear. Helplessness closed Liz's throat. She couldn't handle this. Couldn't watch another person she loved die...

"Liz, listen to me. She isn't dead. The mark we found on her is Shadow, like the one Grey Wolf placed around my wound to keep it from healing. But different. It's that small design on her temple, and Glynn is working on removing it, but it's going to take time and patience. And we need you in control."

"You've come a long way, little Gypsy. There was a time when I was the one guiding you."

Liz felt the wave of love and support coming from their blood-bond and drew it in, absorbing it. She'd missed this. And she hated herself for that. She walked up to Nicolette's unconscious form and brushed the back of her fingers over her cool forehead. A tender gesture, but empty. Nicolette couldn't feel it. Look what caring brought. Pain and loss.

You know better than that.

She ignored the voice in her head. A voice that didn't belong to anyone in the room. "Doesn't this kind of sorcery take time?" Regina's earlier comment to Zander suddenly sprang to mind. "Did you say *Alexei* told you where to find her? How long was she missing?"

"Two days." Glynn Magriel lifted her hands from Nicolette's body, her own shaking with age and exhaustion. "I believe the initial attack left her unable to communicate with any of her blood bonds, and I assume she was kept unconscious and somewhere nearby, to protect her body from sunlight." Lux rushed over to the priestess and led her to a nearby recliner, gently lowering her onto the soft cushions. "With the Shadow Alpha and Grey Wolf dead, I'd believed this old magic passed. I shouldn't have been so ill prepared. I need Mysha."

Mysha, Sylvain's protector while she'd been in hiding all of those years, had been born a Shadow Were, but had proven herself totally loyal to her charge. "Where is she?"

Zander's jaw clenched. "Elder Abaddon will allow no Weres on his property. Not after Sebastian's recent scandal. Neither of Lux's mates, nor Mysha can pass through the doors. And Elder Abaddon has also refused to let us remove Nicolette from this room. He claims as her host he is responsible for her well being."

Finally, she could take some action. "Zander, Regina, take Nicolette and her things back to the loft above Pub Haven. Lux, you and Priestess Magriel get Mysha and meet them there."

"Elizabeth, as the Mediator I have to—"

"No. As the Mediator you have to make the decision that is

Midnight Falls

best for everyone. Best for Nicolette, who is also a member of the Clan Trust. If the Healer needs Mysha to heal these dark marks, then Mysha is what she will have. And I will not allow *that man* to stop me from taking someone from *my* clan, under my care. I will deal with him."

Regina glanced meaningfully at her husband, gathering Nicolette's belongings in silence. She knew there would be no changing Liz's mind. And Liz knew the Reader privately agreed. This was not a place of healing.

Liz felt a shiver run down her spine and turned toward the fireplace mantel before they could doubt the strength of her will. The shuffling behind her meant Regina had talked the Truebloods into doing her bidding, no doubt attempting to prevent the bloodshed Liz was thirsting for. She took a deep breath, preparing to face Malcolm's father, when something caught her eye.

A jewelry box? Carved from one piece of ivory, beautiful symbols adorned the small container, drawing Liz in for a closer look. She picked it up, shock jolting through her system. Why did this seem familiar? Had Malcolm carved this for her—carved and then left it behind when they were turned away from the Abaddon estate? She couldn't shake the feeling that it was meant for her. She slipped it in the pocket of her leather vest before turning to follow a suspicious Zander out of the room, Nicolette limp in his arms.

She'd seen the blood servant go running as soon as they'd begun to pack up Nicolette's things, so she wasn't too surprised by the loud shrieking that followed them down the hallway.

"Whore! Scot whore! You can't take her—you ruin everything you touch. You always ruin *everything.*"

Zander stiffened but Liz just patted his back, nodding toward the others, a silent order to keep walking. She turned to face Malcolm's father. Time had not been kind to Elder Abaddon. His body was bent and frail, the robes that denoted a station he no longer held draped over a body that had lost much of its mass and power.

Liz wrinkled her nose in distaste, and then she studied the blood servant more closely. Abaddon appeared to be starving, but the servant's pallor and fragility indicated he'd been fed from, and recently.

Not that she cared if the old man lived or died. In fact, she'd been imagining new and inventive ways to torture him since the first time they'd met. But her curiosity was piqued. "You look horrible, Pops. And weak. Too weak to deal with someone like me. So just accept that I'm taking Nicolette to get the help you won't let her have here. And I have to tell you…" She lifted her hand to squeeze his paper-thin cheek, winking at the shocked servant beside him. "If I find out you had anything to do what's happened to her. If you are aligned with the Shadow the way your precious Sebastian was—you couldn't pay off enough Werewolves or travel far enough away to be safe from me."

Elder Abaddon stuttered, spittle flying from his cracked lips, his milky blue eyes wild. "N-n-no. *No.* You can't take her. She is supposed to stay here. No one can leave. No one. He's coming. He's coming to kill me. You all have to stay…"

Liz chuckled, an ugly sound that made her wince, yet she couldn't seem to help herself. "If anyone is coming to kill you, old man, I can only guess they have a damn good reason. And you are a fool if you think anyone, least of all me, would stand between you and a bloody end. You chased away the only person who might have, and turned a blind eye to the demon spawn who had him killed."

His head flew back as though she'd struck him. "I had no

choice. He was going to keep looking. Keep digging. It was best for everyone. But now it's too late. He's coming for me."

The servant put his arm around the shaking Trueblood, murmuring gently, in the way a mother soothed a crying babe. Liz turned to start down the stairs, her flippant words covering her shock at Elder Abaddon's response. "Take care of him, I may have questions once Nicolette wakes up. Just don't let him stiff you come payday. You've earned every penny. Oh, and have a steak or two...you both look like hell."

She refused to look toward the closed door where the painting of Malcolm hung, tempting her. Her fingers curled around the small, ivory box as she tried to calm her blood. That bastard had all but admitted what Liz had suspected for years. Sebastian may have believed he was pulling the wool over everyone's eyes, teaming up with a Shadow Wolf to kill the heir to the Abaddon name and prestige, not to mention a seat on the all-powerful Clan Trust. He may have fooled himself, but apparently he hadn't fooled his father.

Elder Abaddon had known Malcolm was going to die. Known and had his own reasons for allowing it to happen. The desire to race back upstairs and watch the life force drain out of his open throat was nearly impossible to resist. Maybe that was why the pain hadn't stopped. Even with the others dead, Mal's father was still breathing stolen air.

But no matter what he'd done to her husband, after seeing him, Liz could hardly believe he had anything to do with Nicolette's current situation. He had looked...broken. She didn't feel the satisfaction she thought she would at that truth.

Because you are too good of a person, my love.

That voice in her head again. "Don't be daft, Malcolm. You were the good one. I'm the bitch. And as loony as your father." How else could she explain the fact that she still talked to a dead man? There may be vampires and werewolves, even giants in the world. But as haunted as she sometimes felt, there were no such things as ghosts.

Chapter Two

Hannah watched the others work from her perch in the far corner of the loft. No one noticed her or invited her into the conversation. They'd moved her sire above the pub—the room Lux had invited Nicolette to stay in when she first arrived. Why had she left this place?

"The Truebloods are fascinating, dearest. They all have such delicious secrets. It reminds me of Venice." Had Nicolette said that only a few months ago? Hannah recalled expressing her concern at Nicolette's mingling with the Truebloods, warning her that even though she'd been accepted into the Trust and given an equal vote, that didn't mean everyone had truly gotten over such a long and deeply felt animosity.

How many times had Nicolette herself told her stories of Unborns who'd been used up and discarded, even killed outright by Truebloods who'd declared their love only hours before?

Even after all these years, the Devas and other Unborns still had to fight for every ounce of respect they received. Had to fight, often for their lives, against Truebloods and Weres who thought they scented weakness. Until a few years ago, most of their challenges had come from the Dydarren Pack, the Weres who lived on the border of their lands.

Jasyn.

It was hard on a girl—becoming a vampire. Especially when she found out the man she'd fallen top over tail for occasionally got hairy and fanged and, more importantly…he *hated* vampires. In particular the one who'd saved her life and was now connected to her more intimately than he had *ever* been. It was more than most women could take.

He'd disappeared for over fifty years, leaving her to discover that absence did not, in fact, make the heart grow fonder. It merely broke it a little more each day, until it was hard to remember when she'd last laughed.

She'd like to think a few years ago she wouldn't have cared that Jasyn Dydarren had found himself in the hands of the Shadow Wolves. But since he'd been back, her heart had started beating again. And since he'd returned from his adventures with Kit and Jesse, he'd actually been…wooing her.

First it was flowers on her windowsill. Yellow roses, her favorite. Then he'd sent her a note wrapped in a faded drawing she'd made for him on one of their first dates. They'd been picnicking by the water and she'd sketched him as he slept on the blanket, unable to control the urge to capture his dark beauty. The note inside merely said, "I still dream of you."

For a Were, he had been remarkably patient. Taking it slow. Irritatingly slow. Nicolette had encouraged Hannah to make him wait, enjoy it while it lasted. She'd said, "Once you're bitten it will be 'Woman. Mine. Mate'. Not that that isn't lovely, but there *is* something to be said for romance."

But Hannah wasn't so sure. The truth was, she wanted to beat him over the head with his love tokens. She was over being angry, over with waiting. If she was his mate, she wanted to be taken. Mated.

Soon after she'd made that decision, he was gone. Sylvain

had come to explain that her husband Arygon had sent his Beta to England to deal with a sensitive matter. A year and a half had passed. The flowers and letters had dwindled, and Nicolette had been less and less forthcoming. Hannah had a feeling that neither one of them were being honest with her.

She knew they weren't having a mad affair, but now it seemed obvious the two had been working on some caper together and decided they shouldn't tell her. She wasn't a fool. They thought her too fragile to deal with whatever it was that was going on. Perhaps that was why Jasyn had always been so hesitant around her. He didn't think she could handle him. Nicolette apparently agreed.

Maybe they were right. When she'd heard Nicolette's mental cry, and then silence, she'd been unsure of what to do. She wasn't Reggie, with her ability to read minds, or Liz, who would know exactly who to hurt and how to do it to get what she wanted or even Madame Nicolette, with her abundance of wit and wiles, and her love of social game play.

Hannah was just Hannah. A youngish Unborn vampire with an inability to fight her way out of a paper bag. It wasn't until Sylvain had showed up on the steps of the castle to inform the agitated Devas of Jasyn and Nicolette's attack that Hannah made her decision. The others would stay behind and hold down the fort. But she had to come here, despite everyone's not so subtle attempts to keep her safe in the castle. A woman closer than her own mother and the man she loved were both in trouble, she had to be brave. Finally.

She looked up from her musings to see Liz and Sylvain arguing vehemently with Lux. The two older women, Priestess Magriel and the Were healer Mysha, had left the room, but the Deva founder and Lux's *grathita* wanted to go after the Weres, to find Jasyn.

Sylvain growled in aggravation at Lux's negative response. "You heard Mysha. She said the mark is part of a set. That means until we find its match we cannot fully remove it. Not without losing Nicolette forever. Jasyn has to have been marked as well. I can find them easily, Lux. You know I can."

Liz nodded sharply. "As can I. I don't have the same control over the elements as your mate does, Sariel, but I had one hell of a mentor. Malcolm was an amazing tracker, you know that. And Jasyn's scent is a familiar one. We are running out of time, Healer. We need to go. *Now.*"

Hannah saw Liz clench her fists, standing toe to toe with Lux Sariel, as she would with anyone who dared to stand in her way. Jasyn deserved a mate with that kind of strength. She was wallowing. She needed to pay attention.

Lux sighed. "Okay, okay. You win. I want Arygon's brother back just as much as you do. But we need a better plan than leap-first-worry-about-safety-later. I will not put any of you in danger. Not with this kind of enemy. Not when there is so much we don't know. Let's talk to Zander."

Sylvain's face softened, and she leaned into her mate. Hannah knew how Grey Wolf had killed Lux's previous lover. Sylvain's own father, the leader of the Shadow Wolves, had almost killed both her and Arygon, reinforcing Lux's overprotective nature.

Liz was not as sympathetic. "You've grown soft with mates and children. You and Zander both."

Lux's eyes narrowed dangerously. "Do not mistake precaution for weakness, Elizabeth. You know the cost better than most. Spend the night here, near Nicolette. Let us do this the right way. Tomorrow will come soon enough."

He led Sylvain out of the room, her attention so focused on

her mate that she didn't notice Hannah huddled in the shadows. Liz paced the edge of the bed, reminding Hannah of a caged jungle cat.

Nicolette had told her once that Liz, for all her tough exterior, was the most vulnerable woman she'd ever known, but it was hard for Hannah to believe. The firebrand with brilliant green eyes and wild, auburn curls, all the more feminine for her skin tight leather pants and shirtless vest—she was the kind of woman you wanted on your side in a bar fight, and far away from your significant other. Hannah envied her.

"Nic, what were you doing in Malcolm's rooms? In Abaddon manor? What kind of trouble did you get yourself into?" Liz sat beside Hannah's beautiful sire, lifting one lax hand in her own. "I should have been here, I should be lying there." A sound like a sob escaped her lips, causing Hannah to bite her lip in surprise. "I'll fix this. I can fix this."

Liz stood abruptly, head lowered as she rushed out the door. Hannah knew she wouldn't let it go. It wasn't in her nature. She would find the answers, find Jasyn and save Nicolette. She should feel relieved, shouldn't she?

"She can't do it alone. It's too big."

Hannah yelped in surprise, falling off the couch to land hard on her behind. Her jaw dropped as she took in the three small, stunningly beautiful children standing above her. Six-year-old Alexei and his three-year-old cousins, twins Rhys and Pax.

She felt a flutter of longing in her stomach at the sight of them. Pax had her mother's silver blonde hair but the Sariel blue eyes. Rhys looked so much like his uncle Jasyn it made her ache. She'd always imagined having his child from the moment she'd first seen him rising naked from Lago Maggiore. A dark fantasy come to life.

Shaking her head to dislodge the vision, she smiled. "Alexei, you scared me. What are you pipsqueaks doing here?"

Alexei held out his hand to help her up, his expression grave beneath his adorable blond curls. "We don't have much time. We are blocking our parents for now. We wanted to talk to you about Aunt Nicolette."

"And Uncle Jasyn." Pax nibbled on her lip, her fingers gripping Rhys's hand so tightly her knuckles were white.

Alexei nodded. "Yes, Pax. And Uncle Jasyn." He helped Hannah back to the couch but didn't let go of her hand. "You have to follow Elizabeth. She will need you."

Hannah's brow furrowed. She'd never met such a grown up child before. "You're blocking your parents? Alexei, I know how close you are with Nicolette. She talked about you all the time. But don't worry. Your mom and dad are working hard to find a way to help her."

He made a sound of frustration. "No one listens to me. You know what that's like. They don't see you either. But they can't help. Elizabeth is going. She'll find them. You have to follow her."

Rhys chimed in, obviously worried. "Alexei said we can save Uncle Jasyn. Then Nicolette will wake up and everyone will stop being scared all the time."

Pax lifted her chin. "I'm not scared."

Hannah smiled at the young girl. "You're braver than I am then."

"She has to wake up if we're going to figure out the secret."

Hannah's gaze jerked back to Alexei's face, his startling eyes so like his mother's. "The secret?"

"The one they were close to when they were taken. And Elizabeth won't be able to handle it alone."

Tears gathered in Hannah's eyes, and she squeezed Alexei's hand affectionately. "I'm the wrong adult to talk to, kiddo. You could probably help Liz far more than I ever could. Unfortunately you have inches and decades yet before anyone will take you seriously. Heck, I've been around a lot longer, and I still haven't solved that dilemma. You said it yourself. No one sees me. I'm not the one for the job."

Alexei smiled, and Hannah felt a wave of power that stunned her. She had a sudden premonition of this boy as a man, with as much power as his mother, maybe more, and the strength to use it as the Sariel heir. "You are the perfect one, Miss Hannah, because you understand and because you belong to Jasyn *and* Nicolette. They are both a part of you, and now, we will be too." Alexei Sariel pulled a small, boy's blade out of his jeans pocket, slicing the fleshy pad of Hannah's hand.

"Ouch! Damn it, Alexei, what did you do that for?" Hannah tried to pull her hand away but Pax and Rhys added their strength to Alexei's. Her eyes widened as he sliced open a wound on each of their hands. The smell of their blood was intoxicating. Power. Sheer, untapped but unmistakable power.

"Our fangs are not developed enough, but this should help." Three small hands slid into hers, their blood gathering in her palm, mingling with her own. Hannah pulled her lips down over her own extended incisors, determined not to frighten the children.

Alexei's smile widened. "Now we can help. Not as much as Mum and Aunt Sylvain. But...it should be enough."

They took their hands away and licked their palms closed, telling Hannah with their big, hopeful eyes to do the same. She lifted her blood-covered hand to her mouth, eyes closing as she drank in the sweet, innocent taste. Strange zaps of energy pinged through her body, images vague and out of focus...and not her own, shimmered in her mind.

The children pulled her from the couch impatiently. "Go. She's made her decision."

Hannah understood. Liz was planning on leaving without letting anyone else know. Planning on searching for Jasyn and the Shadow Wolves herself. She looked down at Alexei and ran her fingers through his silky locks. "You know you're going to be grounded for a hundred years right?"

He wrapped his arms around her in a tight, emotional hug that made Hannah realize that, even with his intelligence and power, he was just a little boy. "It will be worth it."

"Yes. It will." If she could save Jasyn, it would be worth anything.

Even her life.

Three days and thousands of feet of elevation and nothing. The scent of Shadow all over this mountain, mingled with Jasyn's blood told Liz she was in the right place. Montana. What in the name of the Mother were *Les Loups De L'Ombre*, doing in America? But she couldn't deny what her senses were telling her. And she wasn't sure how much longer she could handle the quiet. Where were they? A dozen times she could have sworn she was being watched. Why didn't they attack her already and get it over with? She wanted to kick something's ass, was that too much to ask?

Liz stilled to watch a rabbit scuttle out from its hiding place, and her stomach growled. Not exactly the Were feast she'd been hoping for but she was cold and hungry, and it would have to do. She dropped her knapsack and shifted into her totem form, a black spotted jaguar, and let the animal spirit within her take the lead.

It always baffled her when others had a problem adapting

to the transformation and all of its special perks. Regina for example. She'd taken the young Gypsy away from an incestuous brother, an abusive, narrow-minded father and a life of servitude. Yet when she realized what she was, the girl had chafed against it, mourned for a sun that did nothing but burn your fragile, human skin as you toiled beneath it. Mornings that you woke dreading the pain of the day that was to come. The pain of being a female in a world of men.

She'd come into Malcolm's world with her eyes wide open. He'd never lied to her, and, unlike every other man in her life, he was kind. She'd fallen in love with that kindness. And she'd known what to expect, what she would become, in order to be with him. Although she wasn't his true blood mate, and there were some abilities and connections she'd never share with him, she had no regrets. She'd had this. Her favorite part of what she was. Being freed from the limits of her human body and releasing the wildness lurking within. It wasn't the same, from what she'd been told, as a Were's shift. Vampires had more control. It was less beast, more magic.

She stumbled as her fur was ruffled by a cat racing past her. Strange. She hadn't sensed him coming. He was fast. Too fast. A blur of ebony fur and muscle, passing her and chasing the small, slippery prey away. Damn it. That was supposed to be her dinner. He turned to face her, feline lips lifting to bare his sharp, white teeth. Was he smiling?

He was a beautiful creature. The perfect predator—swift, elegant and deadly. But he was no ordinary feline. Her heightened sense of smell told her he was no more jaguar than she was.

It was strange, his scent. Familiar and yet, like nothing she'd ever experienced. In moments her heart was racing, her body quivering. His demeanor had changed along with hers, his head ducking low, gaze never leaving hers. Was he a rogue

Trueblood? An outcast Unborn? She wasn't sure.

Her senses were scrambled by his arrival. It was anger and adrenaline, not elation, she was feeling. Elation made no sense. Anger at being snuck up on, at allowing someone to get the better of her, was far more acceptable.

Still she had to admit, something about him called to her, grabbed her, demanded she submit. And if there was one thing Liz didn't do, it was submit. She took a slow step back on the rough pads of her animal's feet. He stepped forward, keeping the same amount of distance between them.

Her body tensed in instinctive reaction to his low growl. Arousal, primitive and nearly debilitating, washed over her. An unwelcome and unexpected surprise. She was here for business, not pleasure. She would tell him that if he would shift into his other form and introduce himself, like any other civilized vampire would. The fact that he hadn't made him suspect. Was he connected to the Shadow Wolves behind Jasyn's abduction?

His growl grew louder as though he'd heard her accusation. Her hackles rose and a fine tremor spread through her limbs. The spirit of the wild animal inside her warred with her own common sense. The instinct to give chase, to run with the knowledge that he would have to chase her, dueled with her desire to fight. She'd been in tighter situations. Fought off Shadow Wolves and Truebloods alike without batting an eye. Was she going to put her tail between her legs just because someone's smell got her all hot and bothered?

She ran.

Liz heard the cat's excited grunts as he chased her, purposefully staying a few paces behind. He was acting as though it was a game. *A mating game.* From the way her body was behaving, it seemed inclined to agree.

No. This was crazy. He was vampire, shifted like her. But not like her. Fog descended around her, confusing her. It was him, his power. Like Lux, he controlled the elements with ease. Like Malcolm. He had to be a Trueblood. Not a mark in his favor, as far as she was concerned. The idea of a roll in the grass with the intriguing stranger was pushed out of her mind. She didn't want him *that* badly.

You do. You never wanted anyone this much, my love. Not even me.

Of course I wanted you.

Not like this.

No. Not like this. With Malcolm, after that first attraction to his beautiful face, it was about love and sweetness and—she felt guilty admitting it—gratitude. With all the others through the years it was an itch. A restlessness.

This was desperation. This was need. From his scent alone. She ran harder, through the fog, until her muscles began to shake with exertion. He was running her to ground. A predator focused on his prey. On her.

She turned on him and snarled a warning. No more running. The bastard needed to be taught a lesson. No one made her lose control. She slashed at him with her claws, but he didn't back away, allowing her to cut into his flesh.

Blood. Great Mother, his blood smelled like sin. Like wine and chocolate and hot, sweaty, endless sex. She wanted to taste it, to drink it down, to roll in it. What the hell was going on? Who *was* he?

He took advantage of her distraction, covering her body with his own. She tried to roll out of his hold, but he was too strong. He bit through the black fur and flesh of her neck with his fangs. Not a request, not a wooing, this was a primal domination, instinctual. He was actually delivering a lover's bite. In the form of his totem animal.

"*Not this way.*" She sent him the thought with as much strength as she could, considering her heightened state of lust. He must have heard her, because he started transforming behind her. She did the same, locked in his passionate embrace, pierced by his fangs.

The strong, bare body above hers kept her pinned to the cold night ground. Rocks dug into the tops of her thighs, but she hardly noticed the sting. She couldn't roll over, couldn't see him. Oh, but she could feel him. He was massive, heated, hard muscle. His cock, long and thick, was pressed between the cheeks of her ass, the sensation making her shudder.

The rough hand that wasn't braced on the ground was everywhere—touching her hips, her waist, the side of her breast. He growled against her neck, hips pumping against her and she knew he was as aroused as she was. She told herself it was insane, and it was, but she wanted to please him. This man who shared her animal totem, this man whose face she hadn't seen, who could, in fact have something to do with Jasyn's disappearance, and Nicolette's comatose state.

Liz struggled against her own desire, trying once more to buck his immovable hold. "Not that I'm not enjoying this but—ah, this isn't why I'm here."

He ignored her words, his hips heavy against hers and his hand gripping her hair. He tugged, arching her neck as he continued to feed. His other arm came around her, drying streaks of his own blood from her scratch coating the forearm he pressed against her lips. More a demand than an offering. He wanted her bite.

She could feel the bloodlust coming over her. Her eyes dilated, nostrils flaring at being this close to the irresistible aroma of his blood. It was a temptation she could not deny, no matter how much she wanted to. She bit into his flesh, moaning as his rich blood poured down her throat.

Her body shook against the hard ground as his essence infused every cell in her body, sending her flying into a shocking climax. She sensed his mind entering hers, experiencing her orgasm with her, reveling in it.

"Feel like mine. Taste like mine."

Yes. And he felt like hers. She couldn't get enough. When he lifted her hips, his cock discovering the slick wetness between her thighs, she arched against him. Why wasn't she fighting? Struggling for control? *She* took what she wanted from life, from men. She wasn't some fragile piece to be bent over and taken. Yet here she was, begging for it.

"Yes. Beg. Beg for it."

"You beg. Oh Goddess. Please beg."

His first thrust filled her to her core, her body stretching, struggling to accept him, despite her arousal. *"Please."* His voice was rough with pleasure in her head. He pulled back, the drag of his cock through her clinging sex making him groan. *"Please."* His pleas belied the command of his actions as he powered into her again. So deep that the pleasure mingled with pain. So deep she thought she might die if he left her body.

His bruising grip on her hip tightened to hold her steady as he took her. Her hands clawed at his forearm, tears escaping down her cheeks at the overwhelming sensations of his claiming. No gentleness, just a fierce carnality. Dirty and rough and so intense that she lifted her mouth from his addictive blood to cry out into the quiet night.

Her second orgasm only seemed to spur him on. He lifted himself to a sitting position, carrying her with him until she was on his lap. The new angle gave him the freedom to cup her breasts, to slide his hand down the curve of her belly and further, between the lips of her pussy to rub her clit. His touch burned her skin. Marking her as surely as his bite.

He lifted his mouth, tongue laving her neck to heal the flesh he'd just ravaged. "Ride me." His voice was low and raspy, hesitant as though he wasn't used to speaking out loud. He nuzzled her ear, and she shivered.

She elbowed him lightly in the ribs, smiling in spite of herself when his breath pushed out in a surprised grunt. "Don't tell me what to do."

His fingers slid around her coated sex, circling her clit teasingly. The other hand cupped her breast, pinching her nipple. She felt his grin against her jaw. "Ride me...*please.*"

Goddess his voice was sexy. And he did say please. She tensed her legs, hands gripping his arms as she picked up her rhythm, pressing back against him, filling herself with his thick shaft. He growled his approval, full lips open on her skin.

Her mind reached out to him, searching for the intimacy that the blood connection brought, but all she found was darkness. His feelings were powerful, his thoughts all focused on her. Who he was, on the other hand, was impossible to see. Like trying to make out images through a moonless midnight.

"Midnight."

"What? Midnight? Is that your name?"

"No questions. No questions. Only pleasure. Only this."

His fingers increased their pressure, circling faster against her clit. He slid one finger down to where they were joined, pushing it inside her with his next thrust. "Fuck!"

He dragged it out slowly, lifting the soaking finger up to her lips. "Taste." She sucked his finger in her mouth, and he groaned. "My turn." He pulled his hand away to gather more of her juices, licking his own fingers with a purr of pleasure that made her want to turn, to see him. To kiss him and taste herself on his tongue.

"No." He cupped her chin with damp fingers, keeping her from looking over her shoulder. She was far too aroused to fight him. Speeding toward another orgasm, and she desperately wanted him to come with her. He was close, she could feel it in the tightening of his muscles, his rough breathing, the heated smell of his skin. She craved his release, wanted it more than she wanted her own. It made no sense. She didn't know him, couldn't see into his mind. But some part of her knew him. Knew what he needed, and wanted to be the one to give it to him.

"Yes."

She tilted her pelvis, her hips circling even as she rose and fell against him. Her hand dropped between her legs, caressing herself. She knew he could feel her fingers pressing against her clit, sliding down to circle his cock where it met her sex. A rumbling sound of need came from the man behind her.

"Turn about is fair play. You like that, don't you? Like the way it feels."

"Yes. More."

She tightened around his cock, her sex massaging him with squeezing pulses as she rocked against him. His body jerked against her, and then she was falling forward, on her hands and knees once more as he lost any semblance of control.

"Mine. Mine. Mine."

The mental chant echoed through her head, pounding into her brain to the rhythm of his hips pounding against hers. Deep. Full. Right. He felt...right. Great Mother she was coming. Again. So hard she nearly blacked out with the strength of it. Her body was on fire, soul shattering into a thousand pieces at the same time he shouted with the power of his own release.

His cock throbbed inside her with his climax, filling her until she thought he'd never stop, until their combined arousal soaked her thighs. He left her slowly, and she could sense his need rising again. His regret at separating from her, even for a moment.

He rubbed her back and she pressed her forehead into the dirt, trying to breathe. Trying to think. Her head hurt, a strange ache in her bones, like she'd bruised herself during their passionate tussle.

What in the hell had just happened? She was all for meaningless sex with strangers, but that wasn't what this was. This was like nothing she'd experienced. It was more.

I believe you've just met your match, my love.

Don't be silly. You can't mean what I think you mean.

Grathita...

She was whirled around onto her back, the large, shadowed figure who'd just given her so much pleasure looming over her. "Who do you speak to?" She watched him flinch at the question, but he pressed on. "I heard a male in your mind. Who?"

Liz pushed up on her elbows, her mouth opening and closing, seeking air like a fish that had been ripped from its watery home. She studied the strong jaw line, the sharp cheekbones...a pair of unbelievably blue eyes with a few entrancing flecks of violet. Indigo. Her brow furrowed at the deep, curving scar that ran from the outer edge of his left eye to his chin, and she shook her head.

Her shock must have showed on her face. His expression softened and he lifted her up in his embrace, soothing her with gentle caresses. It couldn't be true. It couldn't be. But apart from the scar... "Malcolm?"

Bright spots filled her vision. She felt like she was going to faint. But she never fainted. It was the last thought she had before darkness consumed her.

Chapter Three

"Welcome to my own personal Hell. Make yourself at home."

Liz groaned, rolling onto her side toward the man sitting with his back to the cave wall. Cave. How did she get here? And where was here? She moaned. Her head was hurting. She ran a hand down her hip. At least she was clothed. Though she distinctly remembered being naked before she passed out. "Jasyn?"

He chuckled, but it sounded a little hysterical. "The jury's still out. You okay? When the Wildman brought you in here I thought you might be dead. You look pale. Paler than usual."

Liz sat up too quickly, grabbing her head as a wave of dizziness crashed over her. "Malcolm."

"No, darling. That man is not Malcolm."

Liz stilled, looking at Jasyn in confusion. "Darling?" She noticed the Shadow's handiwork, a small black mark on his temple matching Nicolette's. Mysha had been right. "Why would you call me that?"

Jasyn grimaced. "I didn't. I told you. This is Hell, and I'm being punished for my sins." His expression changed before her eyes into a sarcastic, feminine smirk that looked eerily familiar to Liz. "*He's* being punished. I, however, am having a delightful time."

Liz crawled closer to the Were, wincing at the bruised, aching feeling in her limbs. Had that sexy vampire dragged her here? "Nicolette is...in your head? But how is that possible?"

Jasyn shrugged. "They knocked me out. Took us by surprise. I know we must have traveled a long way, but I'm not sure how far. When I woke up, I was chained to this wall." He lifted his wrists, jangling the silver metal. "And the lovely dulcet screams of my favorite prostitute were ringing in my ears."

"I was a courtesan. Not a prostitute. I believe we've had this conversation before, Jasyn. It's comparative to the difference between the words civilized and Were."

Liz put a hand to her temple at the unusual argument. "If this is a nightmare I'd love to wake up right about now." She came closer, touching the heavy chains. "Jasyn, you could get out of these. Why don't you just shift?"

He made a face. "Another side effect. I can't. Been trying for days. Neither can Nicolette. We seem to null out each other's abilities. Either that or these chains are made from get-on-my-last-nerve-anium."

"Oh, good, your sense of humor is returning. Lucky us. Liz, darling, you really aren't looking well. I think you need to get out of here. Bring Regina and Sylvain. Tough as you are, I don't think you can handle this beast alone."

It was strange, hearing Nicolette's voice, seeing Jasyn's face. Liz shook her head. "He's no beast. How can he be? He looks just like—"

"But he's not, darling. This is why I don't think you should be here alone. As soon as I saw him, saw how much he looked like the painting of... Elizabeth, you saw Malcolm's body. You told me you watched it burn. Malcolm is dead."

Jasyn nodded. "Whoever *this* guy is, the Shadow Wolves fear him, none of them have come near us since they left us here. I'm not sure what they were hoping he would do. Maybe we were just supposed to be Wildman's dinner. Whatever the case, we definitely need to get out of here. And find a way to bring him with us."

None of this was making any sense. Liz bit her lip as she tried to pull the anchored chains from the wall. Even with all of her strength, she couldn't move them. What *were* they made of? "Has he hurt you?"

Jasyn shook his head. "He hasn't hurt us. Hasn't answered any of our questions either. In fact, from the look on his face whenever we ask him something, your guy doesn't give interviews. He just feeds us, makes sure we're warm, empties our...necessity pot, and checks in to see that we're alive. Other than that, nothing." Jasyn's blush had Liz fighting a smile, in spite of the circumstances.

With five brothers in a one-room cottage, she could still recall how intolerable the lack of privacy was. But to have someone who never left, who was in your head every minute of the day, that had to be hard on a guy. She reached out to squeeze his shoulder in commiseration. "Why do we have to take him back to England?"

A loud, threatening growl froze them in place. Liz turned her head slowly, her gaze stopping on those striking indigo eyes. Malcolm's eyes. He made sure she was watching before his unblinking glare moved to the point where her hand was touching Jasyn. Understanding had her lifting her hand, leaning away from the Were.

The growling stopped.

He was naked. Goddess, he was almost *too* sexy. A dark haired demigod, leaner than Mal had been, harder. And he had a deep, curving scar from the edge of his left brow to his chin. But there was no mistaking the resemblance. The strong jaw, those long lashes, that full lower lip. It was uncanny. Her heart ached for the face she hadn't seen in so long. Her body ached for what they'd shared only hours before.

His brows lowered and she quickly cleared her thoughts, remembering they were connected now. She looked down at his hands. He'd found her knapsack, as well as the rabbit and what looked to be most of its relatives. She held out her hand for her pack. "Thank you. I thought I'd lost it."

He walked past her, still holding her things, and headed to the small fire pit located in the center of the cave. She watched the smoke rise in a steady stream as he skinned and cooked the small animals with fascinating efficiency. The smoke made her think that there must be an opening somewhere above their heads. Another exit.

It smelled incredible. Maybe that was what was wrong. She just needed to eat. It had been a while. She tried not to look at him as he walked over to Jasyn, placing a hunk of charred meat in each of his fists. Jasyn muttered his thanks and strained against his bonds, the chains long enough for his hand to reach his mouth.

They ate in silence. Liz nibbled at her food. It tasted good, but her queasiness hadn't abated. Maybe she was coming down with something. She watched as he tossed the bones into the fire and then leaned one arm behind him, picking up her knapsack to place on his lap. "Who said you could look through my things?"

He was digging into the bag, pulling out her mini travel cooler of synthetic blood, her cell phone and her husband's dagger. He held the last to the firelight, his dark brows lowering at the intricate design. He shook his head, dropping it carelessly on the floor before reaching in to grab something else. The carved, ivory box she'd taken from Malcolm's suite.

She'd handled the beautiful piece a dozen times on her journey, studying the images. On the lid of the box, a carved out thistle made her believe that perhaps it had been a present Malcolm had made for her—his prickly, Scottish flower. The half moon, one of the symbols of the Mother Mal worshipped, seemed more evidence she was right. But how to explain the forms covering the rest of the fragile box? What Liz had originally believed were lovely vines or Celtic knots, were actually snakes, coiled one with the other, waiting to strike. Not exactly a lover's token.

More interesting was this wild man's reaction to it. It fell from his hands, tumbling down his bare legs as he stood up and backed away, as though the snakes had come to life before his eyes.

"Familiar. I know...No! Don't care. Don't think."

"What is it? Do you recognize that?" Liz watched as he closed his eyes, leaning against the wall of the cave without answering. The firelight licked the muscle and sinew of his body like a lover. She wet her lips with her tongue and his cock jerked, hardening before her eyes. She knew he was reacting to her less than innocent thoughts. She looked away, toward Jasyn, who was wearing Nicolette's knowing smile.

"Praise to the Mother, he is a handsome devil, isn't he? It's been cruel, having to watch him walk around naked these last few days." Jasyn grimaced at the words leaving his mouth, and Liz turned in time to see their captor roll his eyes comically. She couldn't help it. It was the first normal reaction she'd seen from him. She laughed.

Midnight, the only name she could think of when she looked at him, opened his eyes wide in surprised wonder.

"Again."

"What?"

"That sound. Do it again."

That sound? "You mean laughing?" Was he so unfamiliar with laughter that it surprised him? What kind of life had he been living here? And for how long? "I'll laugh when I find something funny again. Which, uncomfortable as I'm sure the situation is for my two friends, shouldn't be that long from now."

She walked closer to him, her mind filled with questions. But first things first. "You understand don't you? That there are two of them"—she tapped her head—"inside?"

He nodded, and she smiled. She felt as if she were soothing a wild animal. In many ways, it seemed that was exactly what he was. Though the way he'd made her feel when he'd taken her...she closed her eyes, taking a deep breath. She had to stay focused. "Good. Well, they are my friends. I came here to find them and bring them home so we can heal what's been done to them. Why did the Shadow Wolves bring him here? Can you release them?"

"You want me to let him go because he's yours. The man you speak to in your mind."

"I'm speaking to you in my mind, Midnight."

"Not only me."

He towered over her, his fingers gripping her shoulders to pull her closer to a snarling Jasyn. Liz shook her head at him, her caveman didn't need any further riling. Not by anyone but her. "Let me go."

Midnight ignored her. Curling his lip at Jasyn. "You are safe because you aren't Shadow. I don't kill without reason." He pulled Liz closer to his side. "She is my reason."

"Well, well, well. He talks."

Liz shook her head. "Hush, Nicolette. *She* is a grown ass

woman, you big beasty. Let. Me. Go." His erection was pressed against her hip. Her face heated as she met Jasyn's gaze and saw Nicolette's interest pique. No doubt Jasyn could scent her body's instinctual arousal at his claiming, regardless of her protests. And Nicolette knew everything Jasyn did. Lovely.

"I don't see any stamp of ownership on her, beautiful. Although it's obvious from all that mental chatter that you've...shared something. Are you saying she belongs to you?"

Liz glared. What was her old friend doing? Playing matchmaker while her body lay in the pub loft starving to death? "I thought I told you to hush. Don't give him any ideas, Nic."

"*I already have ideas.*"

"*I know, but mine are better. My friend is sick. Please let them go.*"

"*I'll let them go. After.*"

Her clothes disappeared, and Liz shrieked. Malcolm used to delight in blinking her clothes off at the most inopportune moments. It had driven her batty then, and she wasn't too thrilled about it now. But she was a different woman than the one she'd been. Independent. In control. A bitch. "Don't *ever* take my clothes off without asking again."

He dragged her body against his, his hard cock hot against her belly and she had to admit control was just an illusion when it came to this wild man. There was no denying the power of her feelings, the rightness of his body against hers. She moaned, leaning into him and clutching helplessly at his hips.

"I will not beg you this time." As if he had before. "You are mine. Tell him."

"*Oh, you bastard.*"

"Tell him."

"I belong to no one."

He was too strong, she couldn't resist as he placed her arms behind her back, gripping her wrists with one hand. He looked down, and she watched a long strip of leather appear in his other hand. He tied her wrists together, and she was too shocked to stop him. Not even Kit, her most aggressive lover, had dared this.

"Do not think of another lover again."

His hands moved to her shoulders, and with gentle but unrelenting pressure, lowered her to her knees. He smiled. Dark and wicked, utterly male. It did nothing to ease her discomfort, or her arousal. The warmth of his thighs heated her cheeks, the sight of his cock filling with blood, thickening before her eyes made her mouth water. Her desire for him was a fever that burned rational thought away. Burned her anger away. Without that as her shield, what was she?

"Mine. If you won't tell him, show him."

Jasyn growled at the word. "She doesn't need to show me anything, you son of a bitch."

"The only dog I see here is you." Indigo eyes flashed a warning at the chained Were, before returning to Liz. "I still smell of you, of us. I know you want. Taste me. Take what you want."

She tightened her thighs against the wetness gathering. How could she want him? A stranger who'd pinned her in the forest and taken her like a cat in heat? A man who took away her power? How could she be tempted to do as he asked? And yet, she was. More than tempted. His commanding presence, his expectance that she obey him, turned her on far more than she'd like to admit. His smile faded, but the determination in his gaze intensified.

"Yes, mArjara, *my wildcat. Take what is yours."*

She leaned forward, spreading her legs to keep her balance as she buried her face in the dark curls surrounding his shaft. The smell of his skin, like rich earth and rain soaked forests and him, had her nuzzling closer, making him groan. "Don't tease."

No. She wouldn't. She couldn't. He was her drug. She had to taste him. Her mouth opened and the flat of her tongue glided along his cock, savoring the salty taste, until she reached the tip. She wrapped her lips around the flushed head, glancing up at him from beneath her lashes and leaning forward again to take him deep into her mouth.

His fangs had already extended, a thin trail of blood dripping from the corner of his mouth and down his chin. She sucked harder, focusing on keeping her own need for blood in check, determined to take more before the aroma drove her over the edge. The world fell away. She could feel were the rocks digging into her knees, his cock stretching her mouth and his heart beating in time with hers.

"Take more. Take it all, wildcat. He smells of lust. Show him what he can never have." His words should make her want to pull away, but instead they fueled her on. She felt the head of his cock hit the back of her throat and she swallowed, the muscles tightening around him. His hips jerked, his fist gripping her hair convulsively.

"You make me weak. I would teach him you're mine, but I can't... I won't..."

His thoughts were jumbled, chaotic. He tugged her hair, pulling his cock out of her mouth. He knelt in front of her, covering her lips with his own. The taste of his blood on her tongue had her struggling against her bonds, desperate to pull him closer. Yet, though she could, she didn't break the leather ties. She refused to think about why. She couldn't think. She could only ache for more. *More.*

He ripped his lips away and bent to suck on her breasts. One, and then the other while she arched backward. She leaned on her tied hands, pushing her breasts deeper into his mouth. She felt shameless. Wanting him to have whatever he wanted. Anything. As long as he kept kissing her. Touching her. One of his large hands slid from her back down her ass and between her legs.

Two fingers plunged without hesitation or finesse into her sex, growling against her breast at what awaited him. *"Wet. Mine."* She ground against his hand, needing to be filled with him. So good. But still, it wasn't enough.

"Fuck me."

"Let me hear your voice. Let him hear."

"Fuck me, *please.*"

He gripped her hips and lifted her onto his lap. Her legs wrapped instinctively around him, ankles locking, a part of her afraid he'd change his mind. Afraid he'd stop. Oh Goddess, he couldn't stop. She was too far gone.

He didn't go slow, but she didn't want him to. He wrapped one arm around her waist, gripping her bound wrists with his other hand, causing her to meet his gaze. "Are you mine?"

"Aye, damn it."

"Then bite me." A thrill shot through her at the rough need in his voice. The slice of her gums increased her pleasure as her fangs extended. He tilted his head, his shaggy dark hair brushing against her shoulder at the motion and her mouth lowered to his neck.

Her eyes rolled back in ecstasy at the first, heavenly swallow of his blood. Time slowed as her mind sought his. His heart beat in time with hers, and she sensed a wonder that matched her own at the connection between them. She could also feel his restraint, feel the agonized pain/pleasure as her tight pussy stretched for his cock. *"More. More. Take more."*

She tightened her legs around him, tilting her hips to bring him deeper inside her, eager to obey. They rocked together in a firestorm of need and desperation, as though it had been years instead of hours since they last were joined.

His fist clenched and unclenched around her wrists, his shuddering groans bathing her neck with heat. He pierced her flesh with his fangs, and then she felt him in her body, seeking her mind. She could hide nothing from him. Her past. Her present. Her fears.

Her orgasm crashed around her and she pushed deeper into his thoughts, wanting to share it with him, attempting to see through the dark wall that had stopped her before. Pinpricks of pain turned to sword thrusts. Liz screamed as the horrifying feeling of her mind being shredded, shattered piece by piece sent her hurtling from heaven to hell.

"Why?"

"Get out! Get out!"

Liz lifted her mouth from his neck, falling off him. She broke the leather straps in time to stop herself from landing on her head, her mind reeling, in chaos. She watched him leap to his feet, his hands clawing at his head, heedless of the blood flowing from his temples as he scratched and pulled.

"Stop! You're hurting yourself."

"Can't think. Why did you come? Hurts."

He moved toward Jasyn, eyes closed and one hand outstretched. Liz knew he meant to free the Were as he'd promised, meant for them to leave him to his agony, but it looked like an attack. Jasyn, whose hands were bound, swept Midnight's legs with his own, a defiant growl roaring from his chest.

The man who only moments before had been lost to passion, was now unrecognizable. He rolled off his back into a crouch, his body tensed, ready to strike. Drying blood striped his face like tribal war paint, and his eyes started to glow with a dangerous light. Liz wanted to stop it, wanted to stop his rage and disjointed thoughts from taking her control, but she couldn't seem to break the link. She knew he wasn't thinking clearly. Jasyn and Nicolette would die, and there was nothing she could do to stop it. Even more terrifying, Liz wasn't sure she wanted to. She just wanted the pain to stop.

Midnight pounced, his body curling, claws extended toward his chained target. Liz opened her mouth to scream, praying to Malcolm's Goddess to give her strength.

"Sleep!"

The voice echoed bounced off the walls of the small cave and Liz watched her lover's body crumple midair, falling limply at Jasyn's feet. For the second time in one day, dark spots appeared before her eyes. She. Did. Not. Faint. She slumped to the ground, wondering why the small, blonde pixie above her looked concerned.

"Hannah?"

Had Wildman killed him then? She had to be a hallucination. But as the dust cleared around the fallen vampire, and she didn't disappear, he started to hope. He searched the opening, but didn't see any movement behind her. "Hannah, honey, look at me. Where are the others?"

She seemed to be in a daze, biting her lip as she attempted to tear her gaze away from Liz and the slumped man on the floor. "They're naked."

"Yes, they are." Like anyone needed to remind him. He'd

been equal parts enraged, humiliated and turned on watching the lovers come together, uncaring of their audience. He knew it was the vampire's way of claiming Liz in front of a potential rival. But he soon lost control, forgetting about Jasyn completely. With his dick as hard as a post and Nicolette's wicked commentary running through his head, Jasyn wasn't sure the situation could get any worse. For a moment he understood Arygon's attraction to his own sex. Wildman was pure power, pure Alpha, the way he guided his woman's pleasure. And Jasyn's aggression as he'd lashed out at the lunatic had only increased his arousal.

"I wonder what Hannah would say if she knew you were so kinky."

"It's adrenaline. If you tell her anything—"

"Oh, don't worry, darling. My lips are sealed. Somehow I don't think she'd be able to handle much more excitement right now."

"Thank you."

"I wish I had a witness to that. Jasyn Dydarren thanking me."

Jasyn jangled the chains, every part of him cringing at his helpless position. He may not be able to shift, but even he could sense the danger all around them. Just because the Shadow hadn't approached didn't mean they weren't out there waiting. Without knowing their plans it was impossible to tell.

Now the one woman in the world he most wanted to protect and keep safe was here. And completely distracted by another man's naked body. Not exactly the reunion he'd been imagining. "I think he's already taken, Sheba, but I'm available."

He had her attention now. The last time he'd called her that she'd still been human, and blissfully unaware of what he was. She'd spoken differently then, said it was how everyone talked where she came from. Jasyn had thought it was adorable. Everything about her was. She'd told him Sheba meant a sexy woman. He'd called her that the first time he'd kissed her. The first time she'd come against his hand.

She was biting her lip again, her pearly teeth scraping those perfect bow lips, but this time her eyes were on him. He couldn't let his feelings for her distract him. He had to get them out of here. "Who brought you here, Hannah? And how on Earth did you knock out Wildman?"

"No one brought me here. I followed Liz. And I don't know. Please don't ask me right now. Let's worry about getting you out of those chains and getting out of here."

He grimaced. "I've tried, believe me. Before you ask, I can't shift either. The Shadow's mark has made sure of that. What do you mean *no one* is with you? You couldn't have come all this way alone."

Hannah stepped over the sleeping bodies and came closer, her head down, blonde bob sweeping forward to cover her face. She smelled…edible. She always had. Like a feast made especially for him. His cock grew harder, pressing against the rough fabric of his pants.

She didn't stop until she was standing over him, her small boots planted on either side of his thighs. He lifted his chin and got a good look at her face. Fuck. What had he done now?

"You're in trouble, darling."

Hannah smiled grimly, and Jasyn knew Nicolette was right. "I couldn't have made it here on my own? Is that what you said? You slay me, Jasyn Dydarren, you really do. You're the one chained up and powerless." She leaned forward, placing her hands on the wall above his head. "Your idea that I'm some fragile kid that can't keep up, can't protect myself, can't deal with the *truth*,"—her emphasis on that word made him flinch—

"is bullshit. If you'd just told me..."

She closed her eyes, and his heart twisted. If he'd just told her. What? What he was? That she was his mate? Why he'd left for England, this time? That he'd been helping Nicolette, not only to discover the secret the Abaddon Clan was hiding, but also in an attempt to show Hannah he'd changed?

"All of the above, Beta."

"Stay out of this. I know what I've done wrong. She would have been mine two years ago if you hadn't—"

"I know. Believe me. I was the one cuddling up with the old weasel so you could move around. But she could have been yours long before then, and you know it."

Small pebbles and dust fell on his shoulders, snapping him out of his internal argument. Hannah's beautiful grey blue eyes had left his, looking up at her hands with an expression of shock. He followed her gaze, and his own jaw went slack. The rock surrounding the metal that held his chains in place was crumbling. Hannah's hands were actually sinking into the wall, making it appear as soft as chalk. Jasyn gave an experimental tug and a shout of surprise when the chains, along with large chunks of the wall, came away with ease.

He rolled out of the way of the falling debris, his legs trembling like a newborn pup as he stood. Damn he felt weak. Liz moaned, her eyes still closed, and Jasyn knew it wouldn't be long before she woke, and he had to deal with getting everyone to safety.

He knocked off the stone attached to his shackles, before dragging the chain behind him and heading straight for Hannah. He gripped her arms and pressed her against the cave wall. "Honey, how did you do that?" Unborns didn't have those kinds of abilities. They couldn't knock a vampire out with a word or make the earth move. A horrifying thought immediately sprang to his mind. "Are you claimed, Sheba? Did some vampire make you his blood mate? His *grathita?*" He spit out the word. It wasn't possible. She was *his* mate. But how else could he explain it? And his jealousy at the mere possibility of her being joined to another made it hard for him to think clearly.

So was her skin beneath his hands. Great Mother, how long had it been since he'd touched her, since he'd been this close? "Too fucking long." He mumbled the words against her opening lips, answering his own question before taking her mouth with years of pent up passion.

She kissed him back, a moan of longing vibrating against his lips. He took advantage of her open mouth, gliding his tongue against hers. After a few moments he realized she'd begun to struggle against him, but he couldn't make himself pull back long enough to hear her reasons. He couldn't let her go yet. Just a few more minutes. Or eons.

Hannah had always been his addiction, a constant craving for close to a century. Hell, he couldn't remember a time when he didn't want her so badly his bones ached. And now with one taste he was lost. All he could think of was tasting every inch of her, laying her on the ground and making her his in truth.

He landed close to the fire pit, his breath knocked out of him. It took him a moment to realize what had happened. She'd thrown him. Little Hannah had tossed him across the room. He was weaker than he'd imagined.

"Or she's stronger."

"Don't talk to me."

"Oh! I'm sorry, Jasyn. I just—it's just…I…" Now *that* was hopeful. Jasyn pushed his hair off his forehead, looking at her from beneath his lashes. She was flustered, her cheeks flushed. He inhaled. And not remotely immune to him. She certainly didn't smell like she'd been with another man.

"That's okay, Sheba. I deserved it. I'm sorry." Her startled expression was another punch in the gut. He'd been an ass for so long that a simple apology sent her into shock. He had much to make up for.

Hannah shrugged, shuffling her feet and crossing her arms defensively. "I wish you wouldn't call me that. Anyway, we don't have time for reminiscing right now. I have to get you and Liz out of here before Nicolette..."

"Before I what? Jasyn, ask her. Did they find my body?"

"Where is she?"

Hannah's chin trembled for a moment, and Jasyn had to restrain himself from going to her. He wanted to soothe her, take her into his arms and tell her everything was going to be okay. That he would take care of her. "Where, honey?"

"They took her to her old room above the bar. She, Jasyn, she won't wake up. She won't eat. And I can't hear her anymore. They were talking about hooking her up to an IV when I left."

"She's hurting for you. We should tell her."

"No, we shouldn't. Trust me, darling. Now is not the time."

Hannah walked over to Liz's knapsack, carrying it over to where the Unborn lay, stirring. "We need to get Liz and leave before this other guy wakes up. I don't know how long he'll stay under before we get where we need to go."

"Go?"

"I saw a cabin a few hours down the mountain. No one's been there for a while. It's better than sticking around this cave, and we can stay there until the others come."

Jasyn felt like a parrot. "The others?"

Hannah nodded, rummaging through Liz's things until she

found a pair of leather pants and a vest. "Kit and Lux. They're on the way. I don't know why. I was just planning on having Liz tell me where she hid her plane so she could fly us home. You know, you could be a gentleman and turn around while I get these on her."

He didn't think he should tell her that he'd already seen everything. That he'd watched Liz fuck the man beside her on the floor. That it had made him think of all the things he wanted to do with Hannah. To Hannah.

"Sorry, honey. We can't leave Wildman behind. Strange as it sounds, I think he's connected to the reason we were taken in the first place." Jasyn bent down beside the rough looking man, gesturing to Hannah.

When she came closer, he pushed the man's hair back, away from his neck. Hannah's gasp had him nodding. "We noticed it a few days ago. He's got these markings on both sides. Plus, the bastard looks exactly like Malcolm Abaddon, the hero of the Truebloods. We don't think it's a coincidence. There's more going on here than we thought."

"Why do you keep saying we?"

Shit. "I've been talking to myself for days now. This guy has no conversational skills." Her expression softened, and he knew he'd gotten away with his slip. This time. He should just tell her and get it over with.

"Not yet."

"This delusion you have that you're the boss in this scenario is getting old fast."

"I have no delusions, Dydarren. Just awareness. The kind of awareness that tells me she won't come near you, kiss you, tell you how she feels if she thinks I'm looking over her shoulder."

"Point taken."

Hannah looked down at the two limp bodies and sighed. "I don't know how we're going to get them down the hill, but we should start now or we'll never make it to the cabin by sunrise."

"Agreed. But first," he held up his wrists, swallowing his pride with a grimace. "Can you use those abilities you won't tell me how you got and get me out of these?"

Chapter Four

The scorched scarring started at his collarbone and curved up behind his ear. Intricate loops that reminded Liz of Trueblood Healer tattoos, but sharper, harder somehow. And they weren't the soft, ethereal blue that Lux and Glynn Magriel were covered in. They were black as death.

What had they done to him? Was this why his mind was in such turmoil? And why had they done it in the first place? She rubbed her temples at the sudden, piercing ache in her head. The first time she'd even heard of these dark marks was when Regina had been captured and tortured by Grey Wolf. The bastard had tortured her, then marked her wound, ensuring it would not heal. Now Nicolette, Jasyn and Midnight had all been victims of the Shadow Wolves' special brand of sorcery. The kind that hadn't been around since the war. None of it made any sense.

Liz had woken, clothed once again while she was unconscious, in a small log cabin that smelled of stale human and fire smoke. A hunter's cabin if the trophies nailed to the wall and draped along the floor were anything to go by.

Hannah. She'd followed her here, determined to save her sire and her old lover, regardless of her vulnerabilities. Liz hadn't believed she had it in her. Liz admired her more than she ever had before. The girl had potential.

Not long after night had fallen, she'd had to escape Hannah and Jasyn's presence. Between his silent gestures over Hannah's shoulder whenever she started to mention Nicolette's mental presence, and Hannah's evasion of exactly how she'd suddenly gained her newfound abilities, being locked in with what was bound to be one angry, powerful vampire seemed infinitely more desirable.

She had to hold on until Kit and Lux arrived. Then maybe she could get her balance back. Forget she'd blacked out twice and submitted completely, joyfully to a man she didn't know in front of people whose respect she'd always commanded. She curled up in the chair beside the bed, wrapping her arms around her bent legs, forehead resting on her knees. She felt like shit.

Shame was not an emotion she enjoyed. Not that she hadn't known it before. When her father had declared her a whore and disowned her in the public square, when the Abaddons had mocked and scorned her and thrown their prodigal son out of the house because of her and when she'd had to tell Lux that Malcolm had been murdered.

But this went far deeper. Those were events she could only respond to. Things she couldn't control. This time, she'd given up her power willingly. For sexual gratification. Because he looked like someone she'd loved...no. No that wasn't fair to either of them. It was because she craved *him*.

"*Because you are mine.*"

The graveled voice in her head was gentle, concerned. She turned to watch him as he sat cautiously up in the rickety bed, his eyes alert as he studied possible exits and entries. He shook his head. "We should have stayed where we were. There is no protection here."

"I think Hannah was just happy it had a roof." He didn't

react. He accepted. "Don't you want to know where you are? Who Hannah is? How you got here? Why we—"

"No!" He lowered his voice when he heard the movement in the room beyond. "No more questions, Liz." His nostrils flared, lip curling with apparent distaste. "Liz. That doesn't sound like your name, wildcat. It is far too hard and brittle."

She shrugged. "I'm sorry to disappoint you, but that *is* my name. Elizabeth is too stuffy, Beth is too soft, so Liz it is." She chuckled, lowering her legs as she leaned closer to the bed. "I actually called myself Lisa Marie for a while. I had a mad crush on this rock and roll singer named—*oomph!*"

He laughed as he pulled her over him on the narrow bed. "I told you not to mention your lovers to me, Liz-Beth. I like that. Lizbeth. And you can call me Midnight."

She pretended to huff in irritation, but she was so relieved that he'd woken up in a good mood, despite what had transpired earlier, that she couldn't be angry with him. "My youngest brother used to call me that. You recognized Midnight. I thought it was your name."

He shrugged, undisturbed by his own knowledge. His lack of curiosity was frustrating. But she was beginning to understand why. It hurt him to think, to question. Was that what the marks were about? Did they stop him from finding answers?

He pressed his forehead to hers. "You think too much. It is making you sick. You are mine. Just be mine." She pulled back to study the wounds he'd inflicted on himself before Hannah had stopped him. They'd healed. He smiled softly as she touched his forehead with her fingertips.

Liz felt something start to bloom inside her at his smile. Regina had told her about this, about the connection she'd had with Zander. She could only hope that this wasn't what that was. Unity. She couldn't be his *grathita*. His true blood mate. She was the founder of the Deva Clan. She lived her life by no man's rule. And yet, this man's smile made her melt. Goddess, she had to get away from him before he bit her again. Before it was too late.

It was easy to see he wasn't too happy with the direction of her thoughts. "That Hannah and Jasyn will mate. He does not want you."

Liz snorted. "Gee, thanks. But I already knew that."

"Yet, you fight accepting who you belong to."

"I don't belong to *any*—" They both sensed it. Movement outside. They were no longer alone.

"Hey, Wildman. If you're done playing Tarzan meets Jane in there, I think we've got company." Jasyn's voice drifted through the wooden door, and Liz smiled. Shadow. Exactly what she needed to get herself back on track. A good, honest brawl.

Midnight got to the door before she could blink, shaking his head. "You should stay inside. You are not well."

"Not bloody likely. Just because I've enjoyed what we've done together, does not mean I'll listen to you every time you say jump."

His smile was devilish and she pushed past him to open the door, knowing he could have stopped her if he wanted to. Liz looked him up and down. "You might want to think about pants, lover. Not that the view isn't amazing, but you are definitely distracting everyone."

He looked down as though just noticing his state of undress. Black leather pants, similar in style to hers appeared, covering his muscular thighs. "Better?"

Not for me, she sighed internally.

His smile was blinding. "I heard that."

Jasyn was pacing, agitated. "There has to be a gun in this place. Humans love guns. Especially in Montana." He ripped open drawers, looking for a weapon.

Liz noticed Hannah's surprise. "A gun? What do you need a gun for?" Jasyn clenched his jaw so tight Liz worried his teeth might crumble into powder. For whatever reason, it seemed the Beta was unwilling to let Hannah know that Nicolette's consciousness was having an affect on his natural abilities. And from what she'd seen of Nicolette's ability to communicate through Jasyn, the two had to be in accord. It made about as much sense as anything else had since she'd arrived on this mountain. But there was no time to tiptoe around the issue.

Midnight beat her to it. "Were. If you want to protect your woman you will hear me. It isn't the mark that hinders you. Two minds focused on one task are more powerful than one." The two men stared at each other for long, speaking moments.

Liz just shook her head at Hannah, who was obviously at a total loss. "Don't try to understand them. Just take another swig of that miracle juice you've been drinking because you're going to need it. You wanted to be in the thick of it, and I'm sensing at least ten moving around out there. Maybe more."

Hannah's chuckle was a little hysterical. "A party, huh? I guess we should have stayed in the cave. This is what I get for listening to a kid." Liz raised a questioning brow but Hannah just waved her off, her head tilting as though listening to something.

Liz heard it too, a scuffling on the roof. Midnight strode toward the door. "Time's up." He whipped it open, and she watched the thick fog roll in with the night air. "I'll be back." And he was gone.

"Damn Trueblood show off." Jasyn mumbled beneath his breath. He inhaled deeply, his hands curling in concentration.

His growl was a painful sound. Liz held her breath as he started to shift into his Were form. The sound of his shirt rending and joints popping was drowned out by the first screams of the Shadow outside. She had to get out there. Had to help Midnight.

She gripped Hannah's shoulders. "Stay with Jasyn. Protect each other." She took a deep breath, trying to ease her nausea before she leapt into the fog, shifting mid pounce. Her jaguar's paws hit the ground running, searching for her mate. He was close, fighting. She could smell his blood.

Whoever touched him would pay.

A large, clawed hand dug into the scruff of her neck. Shadow Wolf. She hadn't seen him, too determined to get to Midnight to be aware of her own safety. The Were flung her against a tree, and her scream of pain echoed through the fog. Why was she so weak? She stumbled to her feet, lunging toward the retreating beast's back. Luckily her aim was true, and her strong jaw clamped down on his throat, reveling in his garbled snarl of pain as she bit through thick muscles and hit bone.

The blood poured down her throat, bitter to the taste, filled with dark thoughts of death and the need to kill him. Midnight. Satisfaction came when she felt his body cease its struggle, falling to the ground with her fangs still embedded in his neck. She lifted her head and licked her chops, attuning her senses to the scuffling movement in the fog.

Five more Shadows surrounded her, some in human form chanting low, some in their werewolf forms waiting for the opportunity to strike. Their chant was burrowing into her head, making her dizzy, immobilizing her. She had to stop them. Had to stop. But why? Why was she fighting them? Why, when all she wanted to do was lay down and let them pass?

"*Lizbeth!*"

Her drooping eyelids lifted in time to see someone cut through the fog. Midnight. He snapped the neck of the human Shadows, so hard she was surprised their heads didn't separate completely from their bodies. With the chanting stopped, Liz could feel her focus returning. She barely had a chance to snarl at the remaining Were before the eerily calm Trueblood ripped their hearts from their chests, tossing them to the ground beside their crumpling bodies.

"I told you to stay inside."

"I've fought Shadow Wolves before. I can hold my own."

"I can see that. You are a lot of trouble, wildcat. I may have to tie you up again."

Images of the last time he'd bound her wrists, and the pleasure that followed made her body shudder. "*Unfair, Midnight.*"

"Stay alert. I'll be right beside you."

She kept her mind linked with his, amazed at his unusually heightened senses. Every vampire and werewolf had an intensified sense of smell, sight and hearing. Their instincts were far superior to humans. But Midnight's abilities surpassed even Malcolm's. Through him, Liz knew there were eighteen Shadow Wolves surrounding the cabin, one very near the open door. Hannah and Jasyn were still inside, Hannah doing her best to protect the struggling Beta as he changed.

She also sensed others. Weres but not Shadow, they were stealthily making their way down the mountainside to their location. Midnight sent her soothing thoughts. He knew them. They had come to help.

All of this information came to her in seconds. Liz turned back toward the cabin to take care of the Shadow headed toward Jasyn. If something happened to him, Nicolette would be lost to them forever.

She lashed out with extended claws, slicing the backs of his knees and dropping him to the ground. Glass shattered, and Hannah screamed. Liz looked up from the wounded Shadow in time to see another Were dragging the young Unborn through the window on the other side of the cabin.

Jasyn, still trapped mid shift, went wild. He'd found his motivation. In moments he fully shifted. The large, dark werewolf leapt through the window after his mate.

"Don't touch the black one, he's still of use to us." She heard the shouted order and turned toward the voice. Another unshifted Shadow. She sent her thoughts to Midnight.

"We need that one. Need to find out why they did this to Nicolette and Jasyn."

"No Shadow will be left alive."

"Damn it, Midnight."

"You may drink his blood first."

"Fuck."

She arrived in time to see Midnight appear behind him. The Shadow saw her and began to chant immediately, dark ancient words of power that wrapped like a ribbon around her. Midnight's hand snapped out quickly to grab his tongue, changing the words into a shriek of agony as he tore the appendage from the Shadow's mouth. Liz gagged, feeling a tremor of fear as she looked into emotionless indigo eyes. Not for the first time she wondered who this man was.

"I am your mate. Discover what you need to know. Now."

There was no time for hesitation. Liz bit into the squealing Were's neck and drank, opening her mind to the knowledge in his blood. He only knew two things. The Shadow who captured or, preferably killed the man with the face of the Storm Bringer would be the new Alpha of the scattered Shadow Wolves. And the Were they'd marked could not be killed. Not yet. Not until they had what they wanted.

The Storm Bringer. Did he mean Malcolm? A fleeting thought that he had failed and the flash of a familiar face was the last Liz sensed as Midnight pulled the limp body from her reach and snapped its neck. She heard the loud howls and knew the other Weres Midnight sensed had arrived.

Liz saw a small, brown wolf race by, knowing it was Hannah, with three Shadow Wolves barreling after her. A jet-black Were dropped in front of them from above, his eyes gleaming with bloodlust.

The Shadows backed away, attempting to circle him, and Liz knew their orders made them hesitant to injure Jasyn. A fact he took full advantage of. His large clawed paw slashed out at the largest Were, ripping deeply into the flesh of the Shadow's muzzle.

Growling warnings at Jasyn, they inched closer. He bared his teeth and the three dove on him, rolling across the rocky forest floor, a bundle of snapping fangs and struggling bodies. Liz stepped forward to help, but Midnight held her back.

"He must do this on his own."

"There are three of them."

"He protects his mate. And the others are watching."

Liz noticed the fog clearing, realizing the three Shadow Wolves struggling with Jasyn were the last left alive. But they were not alone. A few nude men and several large timber wolves were standing in silent observation, seven in all, watching Jasyn fight off his attackers.

Jasyn, weakened by the Shadow's mark and his connection to Nicolette, was smaller than the Weres attacking him. His fur was matted with blood from their sharp fangs and claws. They could see he was at a disadvantage, and yet they did nothing to help him. And Liz could clearly see Hannah being held back by the watching wolves, ensuring she wouldn't rush in to help or distract the struggling werewolf.

"Macho posturing. He could be killed, and you men are all just standing around watching. Like it's a game."

"Then he will be killed in the defense of his mate. Honorably. But he is stronger than you think, wildcat. Not everyone needs you to save them."

As if in response to Midnight's faith in him, Jasyn flipped the Shadow Wolves over, rolling to his feet. They scrambled after him, all thoughts of caution gone now, replaced by the need to kill. The need for blood.

Liz had to admire Arygon's brother. She'd underestimated his fighting skills. Even against the frenzied Shadow, the Beta was more than holding his own. He was making them look like untrained pups. Playing with them. One by one they fell, until a single Shadow, the biggest of the group, remained.

With blood dripping from his face from Jasyn's initial blow, the Shadow shifted into human form. Broad shouldered and handsome, claw marks already healing on his body, his smile was conciliatory. He took a step closer to the alert Were. Shocked murmurs went through the crowd, and Liz too was surprised. What was he doing?

"The old Healers will not be able to remove the mark. You will be trapped with the vampire whore inside your head until she dies from starvation...or you go insane. If you come with me now we will leave the others alone. We are the only ones who can help you."

Jasyn hesitated, his gaze instinctively seeking Hannah's wolf. The Shadow's expression grew confident. "She's yours, I can see that. We will protect her. It isn't her fault she's Unborn. Those poor accidents aren't who we're after. Come with us, and she'll be—"

The handsome Shadow stopped speaking abruptly. No doubt due to the clawed fist buried in his chest. Howls of triumph filled the air as he fell to the ground. The dark Were had been victorious. Jasyn stumbled a bit, before throwing back his head and joining the chorus.

Liz sighed. Men.

"Are you okay, Liz? You aren't looking well."

Liz rolled her eyes at Hannah, her arms wrapped around her body, shivering in the cool mountain air. "If anyone else says that I'm going to kick their ass." Where was he? The night was nearly gone but Midnight was still walking the perimeter. If she couldn't sense his amusement at her impatience, she'd be worried. As it was she was just pissed that he'd left her with these American Weres.

"Did you know about these guys?" Hannah's lowered voice beside her sounded fascinated, and not a little nervous. Vampires and werewolves didn't hang out as a rule, and yet, these Weres had shown no outward animosity to Hannah or Liz, quite the opposite.

When the dust had settled from their fight with the Shadow, they'd been invited to join their new friends for dinner on the other side of the mountain. Nothing could have surprised Liz more than discovering a werewolf compound, teeming with women and children, all of them ready with friendly smiles. Strange Weres indeed.

She shook her head at Hannah, scratching the painfully sensitive skin behind her ear. "No. I bet the Shadow were as surprised as we are. I'd never heard of any clans or packs in North America. And I'm pretty sure Arygon didn't know about them either."

"The Were Alpha? Dydarren's been telling us about him. No, I'm guessing he doesn't know about us. Can't say I'm too eager for him to find out either. We aren't real sticklers for rules or bosses around here." Liz couldn't help but admire the stunning Were and his easy manner. A lean, long legged man, a cowboy hat covered his short blond hair, his tan face creased with laugh lines. He was straight out of a western romance novel.

His dimple deepened as though he sensed the direction of her thoughts. "I wanted to introduce myself. I'm Wyley. And *you* are friends with our resident bogeyman. Which might just make you the most interesting visitors we've had in a dog's age."

He laughed, and Hannah joined him, but Liz felt her hackles rise. "Bogeyman?"

Wyley held up his hands in self-defense. "Just a joke, ma'am. He's been around longer than I have, and there are only a handful of us who claim to have seen him once or twice. He's a legend. The jaguar that protects the mountain. The Cursed One."

Hannah's brow furrowed. "Cursed?"

Wyley nodded soberly. "My great grandfather claimed this land a while back with his mate and a few other families. Story is he'd come here because he was tired of the constant battle for supremacy, the fight for land. He came here thinking with all this splendor, there'd always be enough room for human and Were alike." He shrugged. "The world's filling up, but we have this mountain mostly to ourselves. Except for the Cursed One. My favorite bedtime story told about a vampire who appeared out of the fog, his body bruised and marked with an evil curse. His punishment for his sins was to remain on the mountain, and keep us safe from others of his kind." He smiled. "It's only a story, but he has definitely helped our families out more than once, though he never stayed around long enough for us to thank him."

"Cursed One, huh? I bet you liked being called that."

"Midnight is better."

An older woman walked up to Wyley, smiling shyly at Hannah. "Jasyn Dydarren asked me to see to your comfort, Miss Hannah. We have a room for you to freshen up in, some clean clothes, and the men are putting together a late night barbeque with the trimmings to celebrate your arrival."

"I've missed American hospitality." Hannah smiled at Liz and Wyley before following the chattering woman back the way she'd come. Liz shook her head. She missed having control. Over anything. Here, up seemed to be down, and black was white. Jasyn was Nicolette, and Liz was a sexual submissive to a cursed caveman. She missed Deva castle. And she really needed to find Midnight before she fell over. Maybe he could make her feel better.

"Don't let him bite you again."

"Regina?"

"You're sick, Liz. More than you know. Lux is coming. Wait for Lux."

Regina's voice faded, the ringing in her ears blocking her out. Great Mother her head hurt.

Wyley dipped his head to get her attention. "Dydarren mentioned something about more of you coming. Did I hear him right? Is one of them a real live giant?"

Liz laughed, covering her discomfort with a smile. "You're a real live werewolf. Why should a giant shock you?" He blushed and she laughed harder, utterly charmed. If he was an example of the other Weres around here, she might have a hard time disliking the furballs. "Don't worry, Kit is a good guy. He and

Jasyn are friends."

"Come to me, wildcat. Before I have to fight the pup as well as this giant you have fond feelings for."

She thought about resisting for a moment but she'd been longing to see him again. She hopped off the small garden fence she'd been sitting on, wobbled a bit, righting herself to head toward the outer doors of the compound. "Save me some of that barbeque. I'll be back soon."

She walked slowly into the tree line, reaching out with her senses. *"You know, it's rude to stay out here when you've been invited inside."* She jumped when she heard a rustling behind her. Nothing was there.

"I don't belong inside. It's safer for everyone this way."

"Of course you belong inside." She thought about what it would be like for him. The curiosity of the children. The questions. And she thought she understood. How long had he been alone out here? A few hundred years at least. The Cursed One. She was surprised he hadn't gone insane.

"Your scent drives me insane. The taste of you. The feel of you coming around my cock. Your bite."

Liz stopped, unable to move as a rush of desire raced through her limbs. Goddess, her need for him was stronger than before. How was that possible?

He's your grathita. *What I could never be, he is. Why are you fighting it?*

Large hands slid beneath her arms and pulled her up into the trees. Midnight. She was breathless by the time he set her down in front of him on a thick, sturdy branch. He caressed her cheek with his rough fingers. "The voice. It's a memory."

"Yes."

"The memory makes you sad. Makes you regret."

"Sometimes." Liz hastily brushed a tear away as it escaped down her cheek. "Sometimes it makes me face things I don't want to."

He leaned his forehead against hers. "You're sick. I should take you back. I wish I could..."

She felt the pain this line of thought was causing him, and pressed her fingers to his lips. "Shh. Let's do this your way. No thinking. No more talking." She replaced her fingers with her lips, kissing him with all the pent up emotion inside her.

"Make me forget."

"Mine, wildcat. You're mine. That you must always remember."

She felt the cool breeze on her naked skin and smiled. Yes. This was what she needed. This would make her feel better. She wrapped her legs around his waist, lifting up until she was straddling his lap. Her damp sex pressed against his hardening shaft and she purred, loving the feel of him against her.

His hands slid around her hips to grip her ass, squeezing, caressing. She lifted her mouth. "Aye. Take me there."

"I love it when you say that."

"Aye? I can't concentrate when you're touching me. Oh, do that again."

She rubbed herself against him, coating his cock in her arousal, and he growled, his cheeks flushing, eyes brilliant as they gazed into hers. He was trying letting her set the pace. In his own way, trying to give her back some of her lost control.

And how she loved him for it. His hands tightened on her skin at the thought, but she shook her head, taking his mouth to distract him. No thinking. Only feeling. One of his hands left her hips, and she felt his fingers exploring her sex.

He kissed her cheeks, her chin, her neck. His lips followed

a path to her breast while his fingers filled her, fucking her. She arched into his mouth, his hands, lost to sensation. Only when she felt his extended fangs scrape across her nipple did she regain awareness long enough to push him away. "No biting this time." A sound of disagreement rumbled in his chest, but she had to stay firm. Maybe she was using Regina's warning as an excuse for not being able to face what would come after. She couldn't handle sickness or Unity. Not right now. "No. Biting."

She could tell he was tempted to question her, but instead he lifted her off his lap and turned her until she was gripping the thick bark of the tree. She gasped at the scrape of the wood against her skin, and Midnight's hands spreading her cheeks.

One blunt finger, still damp with her juices, pushed through the tight muscles of her ass. "Great Mother, aye. Please."

"You want me to fuck you here? Fill your sweet ass with my cock?" He gripped her hips and dragged her closer. Liz shouted in pleasure as the wood scraped her sensitive nipples. The head of his cock replaced his finger. "Is this what you want, *mArjara*?"

"Yes."

His carnal excitement fueled her own. She took a deep breath, trying to relax her muscles as his thick shaft stretched her inch by overwhelming inch. This is what she wanted. What she needed.

She clawed at the bark, moaning at each slow, drawn out thrust. Her fangs extended, nicking her lip. She licked the blood and closed her eyes, yearning for his taste in her mouth.

"Tight, wildcat. So good. Tell me what I want to hear."

"I'm yours. Harder, Midnight. Fuck me harder."

"Mine. Mine to fuck. Mine to bite."

"Yes. No. No biting."

The leaves around them quaked, fluttering to the forest floor below with the power of his thrusts. He wrapped an arm beneath her breasts and lifted her up to lean against his chest. The position pushed him deeper inside her.

"Before I'm through you'll beg me to bite you."

Chapter Five

Heaven must be filled with scalding hot showers. After days of dirt and bugs and fresh air, Hannah had wondered if she'd ever feel clean again. She was *not* a nature girl. Never had been. The irony of falling in love with a Were, a species full of wilderness junkies, was not lost on her. But then, she hadn't known what he was until it was too late.

At least these Montana Weres had their priorities straight. And they were kind, not even a hint of superiority even though she knew they were aware of what she was. It felt like coming home. Though her home was a few thousand miles away. California.

Growing up in Hollywood during the twenties, she'd thought she had it all figured out. The world was her playground. She would travel it alone and make a name for herself in Europe as a great artist.

She had wanted to see everything, do everything. But first she had to get there. Her mother's family was from a little town on a lake called Maggiore, so she had told her aunt that she wanted to learn about her roots. The elderly woman had doted on her, her last surviving relative other than Hannah's younger brother, who she didn't acknowledge because of his hard boozing, criminal ways. She'd given her enough to get there and back, and made Hannah promise to write her a letter from the town of her grandparents' birth.

She'd only meant to stay a day. Mail the postcard and head for Rome. But the artist in her was lost from the moment she'd set foot in the tiny village. It was as though she'd walked into a painting. Everything was perfect. So it hadn't surprised her when he appeared.

Jasyn. She'd played the what if game a million times throughout the years. What if she hadn't gone looking for him that night demanding he tell her why he refused to introduce her to his family? What if she hadn't crashed that borrowed jalopy? What if she'd become his mate instead of an Unborn?

But it had all happened, and he had changed from sensitive lover to cruel stranger. And now, now he was looking at her the way he used to, but he was holding something back. Still not telling her everything. Then again, she had her secrets too.

Who knew such a small blood exchange could make this kind of difference? Alexei and the twins were so young, and their power was already unimaginable. She'd felt them with her, guiding her when she could no longer sense Liz on her own.

When she'd seen the strange vampire apparently attacking Jasyn, the power had flowed not from her, but through her to put him to sleep. The chains too. It scared her, that she was doing these things. Especially since she couldn't communicate with the children the way she had always been able to with Nicolette. All she had were vague feelings, or sudden knowledge, like the awareness that Kit and Lux were on their way to help, and that they'd been apprised of the current situation.

Those kids were something else. She wished they'd tell her how to deal with her feelings for Jasyn. There'd hardly been time to talk with all the excitement, but that moment in the cave when he'd kissed her told her all she needed to know. She was still stuck on him.

Nicolette would know what to do. There wasn't a woman alive who knew more about men than she did. Of course, she'd had a lot of practice. But considering the current situation, a situation that had suddenly become a lot clearer during Jasyn's fight with the Shadow Wolves, she wouldn't be having that confidential girl talk anytime soon. She would just have to figure out how to get that pain in the ass Were alone, and maybe get another chance at that kiss.

"Our hostess Amy didn't want me to tell you, but people are beginning to wonder whether you're a vampire or a mermaid. How long are you planning on staying in that shower anyway?"

Hannah smiled, watching his blurred frame coming closer through the steamed up shower door. "As long as the hot water holds out. It's wonderful in here. This may be the best shower in the history of indoor plumbing. And it's so roomy."

Silence. Then she saw his hands reach for the buttons of his shirt. "Bold claim. I may have to test it. Just to be sure you're not exaggerating."

Her stomach fluttered, skin heating from more than just the water temperature. This was exactly what she wanted. But she wanted it on her terms. "Slow down, Dydarren. I don't think I extended an invitation. Yet."

"Yet?"

"First, you're going to answer a few of my questions. For every one you answer honestly, you can remove a piece of clothing. Deal?" She held her breath as he considered her offer. *Please say yes.*

"Deal. But don't take too long." His voice was lower, gruff, and her thighs tightened in anticipation. She was just as impatient as he was, but there were a few things she had to know.

"Why did you leave this time? What were you working on with Nicolette?"

She peered through the steam, watching him unbuttoning his shirt as he answered. "That's complicated. I didn't want to leave. I was…in the middle of something back at home." She knew what he meant. "But Arygon asked for my help. Not long after Nicolette arrived in England and was given permission to peruse the Clan Trust records, a history of rulings as well as the minutes of every meeting, she found anomalies."

"Anomalies?" Hannah swallowed. His shirt was gone. She could see the dark hair on his chest and her hands curled on the glass, aching to touch him.

He nodded, leaning against the sink to remove his borrowed boots. "References to a fanatical group within the Trueblood community. A group who thought a lot like our old friend Sebastian Abaddon, who believed that the rules created by the Trust hindered the race. They'd reached their peak before the Great War between the Truebloods and Shadow, and apparently a few of the elders believed they might have had something to do with it. One or two even thought some of their own members were involved."

Trueblood elders involved in starting the war? She'd always thought that the Shadows forced the confrontation. She wiped the moisture off the shower door so she could see him more clearly. "Why did she need your help?"

"I was a distraction mainly. A Were hanging around Haven and sticking his nose in where it didn't belong was highly distracting for the Truebloods." She heard the wry humor in his voice. "I also kept watch on Abaddon keep after she moved in there. She'd light a candle every night at a certain time, and I'd know everything was all right. She didn't want Regina or the Mediator to know that she was worried. I guess she knew no one would suspect the two of us of working together."

"She trusted you." He shrugged, his hands on the top button of his jeans. "What are you waiting for?"

Jasyn smiled tightly. "Your next question. I'm following your rules, Sheba, but my patience is wearing thin. Is there anything else you want to know?"

She slid the door open with a bang, the steam parting to reveal her naked and trembling body to his gaze. "Why didn't you make love to me? I understand why you left after I'd changed. I know what happened between Nicolette and your family. I mean before. You touched me, kissed me, but you rejected me when I offered more. If you wanted me so much, why?"

He swallowed hard, his gaze on her small, firm breasts, her pale skin. "I wanted you too much, Sheba. You have a better idea now of what mating means to my species. I knew from the moment I smelled your scent on the wind that you were mine. I'd been so angry, at everyone and everything, but you took it all away with a single smile."

She gripped the door until her knuckles went white, wanting to comfort him, wanting him to tell her everything. He unbuttoned his jeans. "I could have bitten you that first day, taken the choice out of your hands hoping the chemistry between us would be enough. But I wanted you to..."

"Love you?" He nodded, his eyes closing in remembered anguish. "I was walking along the shore where we'd met, trying to work up the courage to tell you what I was, how I felt. I didn't reach you in time. You would have died, but I was too angry to be thankful. Too much of an ass."

"You're still an ass. I guess the only question left is, are you thankful now?"

He came forward, not stopping until she was pressed

against the far wall of the shower, the hairs on his chest tickling her sensitive nipples. "Oh, Sheba." He wrapped her wet hair around his fist and tilted her head back. "Never doubt it."

Her body melted against his at the possession of his kiss. This was what she remembered, what she'd waited for. The man she'd fallen in love with. Her mouth opened to his tongue and his taste pulled a moan from deep in her chest. Too long. It had been too long.

She rubbed his shoulders, his back, her leg lifting to tangle with his, desperate to feel more, to get closer. He lifted his mouth, his breath shallow. "Hannah, wait. You have to know before we go any further. Nicolette...she..."

She hopped up, twining her legs around his waist so his erection was pressed against her sex. "I know for a fact she's experienced a threesome before. Just tell her I can't wait any longer, and kiss me." She watched as what she said hit him. The awareness that she'd figured out what he wasn't telling her, that she knew that he was sharing his consciousness with Nicolette because of the Shadow's mark and she didn't care.

"Anything you say, Sheba." He lowered his mouth to hers, growling when she took his lower lip between her teeth and tugged, licking the wound with teasing flicks of her tongue. "Don't tease me, honey. I need you too much."

She lowered one arm, wrapping her small fist around his cock. "No teasing," she panted. "Not this time." Her legs tightened around him, feeling his muscles tense and flex with that first, powerful thrust.

"*Fuck.* Great Mother, Hannah, I knew...knew you'd feel this good around me. Holding me so tight, honey. So *tight*..."

"Oh, Jasyn. Yes, harder. Fuck me harder. Make me take it. All of it. *Yes.*" She knew she was screaming, but she couldn't think, couldn't care. He was here. Finally. And reality was better than the nights she'd spent alone, touching herself, imagining his hands, his mouth on her body.

He gripped the small window ledge above her and spread his feet, bracing himself as he slung his hips hard against her, jarring her body with every pounding thrust. And she loved it. Loved his lack of control, his wildness.

He bent his head to suck one nipple, then the other, deep into his mouth. He pulled back and she could see his eyes changing, his canines lengthening. Her own fangs had extended from her gums. She craved his blood. She needed to be inside of him. To taste him. He shook his head, closing his eyes even as his hips increased their speed. She cried out and he bit his own lip, drawing blood. "I love hearing you call my name, Sheba. Love to hear your screams as I take you."

She licked the blood from his lip, moaning in delight at the addictive flavor. "Bite me, Jasyn. I'm so close. So close. Bite me and make me yours."

He slammed his hips so hard against hers the tile behind her cracked. So hard she couldn't hold back her shout of pleasure. "You *are* mine, Hannah. Mate. You've always been mine."

He came with a roar and she followed him into oblivion, loving his passion, trying not to feel rejected by his refusal to bite her. He kissed her forehead, leaning his own against the tiled shower wall. "When I bite you, there will be no going back. And I want to be the only one in my head when my heart joins with yours."

She nodded against his shoulder, kissing flesh already chilling from the freezing water. "We should probably get out of here."

A pounding on the bathroom door startled them. "Kit and I are really glad you two finally got together. Sounds like it went well. But you're scaring the werewolves, and I need to know where Liz is right now, so we need you to come on out of there. The sooner we get everyone home the sooner I can get back to *my* mates."

They looked at each other and started to laugh, saying his name in unison. "Lux." Hannah couldn't find it in her heart to be embarrassed. She was too...happy. From the glow in Jasyn's eyes as he turned off the shower and dried her off, he felt the same.

"This is delicious barbeque. Jesse will be sorry she missed it." Kit bit into yet another large turkey leg, much to the fascination and delight of the Were children watching every move he made. Apparently, word of what he was had spread through the small community like wildfire. The younger kids had been peppering him with questions.

"You don't look like a giant."

"I get taller."

"Taller? How tall? Can you get as tall as that tree over there?"

"Yes."

"Wow."

Jasyn smiled and shook his head, looking over at Lux. "I was the hero for about five minutes before he arrived. But kids are all the same. Who can compete with a giant?" He would never admit it, but he was glad Kit had come. He'd grown close to the Sariel guard over the last few years, considered him a friend.

Lux chuckled, licking the sauce off his fingers with obvious delight. "Too true. I could rain lightning down in the middle of this party, and they'd still want to see him grow." He elbowed

Jasyn, directing his gaze toward Hannah, her hands animated as she talked with the women of the compound, asking if anyone had seen Liz. Jasyn shouldn't be surprised that he wanted her again. A part of him resented Lux, even though he'd come to heal him. Even Kit, though he knew the Igigi had come to help. He just wanted the world to stop so he could make up all the time he'd lost with Hannah.

"For a Were you are fond of your courtship, aren't you? Arygon could learn a lesson or two in romance from his younger brother."

Jasyn shook his head. "Arygon goes after what he wants. That's why he was born to be an Alpha. He didn't wait eighty years to claim his mate. Mates," he corrected himself. "And I'm *still* waiting because of those damned Shadows. Think you can heal this?" He tapped his temple.

"Darling, you really shouldn't beat yourself up about it. From what I saw, our Hannah isn't holding any grudges."

"She's talking to you now, isn't she?" At Jasyn's nod Lux grimaced. "No offense, Nicolette, but I can't imagine a worse fate for a man set on claiming his mate to have the equivalent of a mother-in-law privy to all his intimate thoughts."

"Thanks for pointing that out, man."

"Anytime, Dydarren. We're family after all." Lux glanced over at Hannah again. "She told you about my children's part in this didn't she? That Alexei, Pax and Rhys ganged up on her and led her right to you. Leave it to Zander's heir to lead my innocent children astray."

"Alexei? They must have exchanged blood with her. That child is too brilliant for his own good."

Jasyn could only agree with Nicolette's assessment. "Why did they put her in that kind of danger?"

Kit joined them, shooing the children away with the

promise of showing them his ability tomorrow. "Jesse says even her father admits to being wary of Alexei. He's powerful. And smart. He wouldn't have done it if he didn't believe Hannah could help. He loves Nicolette. And his cousins love their Uncle Jasyn. They wanted to help."

Wyley loped over to them, cowboy hat firmly in place. "Don't mean to eavesdrop." He chuckled. "Actually that's exactly what I meant to do, but you understand, I have to keep me and mine in mind first."

"Understandable." Jasyn's nod welcomed him into the small group.

"He can spy on me anytime."

"Great Mother, why do you hate me?"

"She doesn't hate you, darling. If anything, I'm the one being punished. My body is rotting in England, when I could be bucking with my very own bronco right here."

He rubbed his temples, and Kit's expression was sympathetic. "We appreciate your hospitality. We didn't mean to drag innocents into this."

Wyley's smile was broad. "It certainly seems more exhilarating in your neck of the woods. The most excitement we have is the occasional militant hunter. Or a sighting of the Cursed One. We know good folks when we see them…and bad. If you need any more help with those Shadow Wolves, we're in."

"I may be in love."

"Shut up!"

Lux laughed at Wyley's offended expression. "He doesn't mean you, Wyley. That mark on his temple is just giving him one hell of a headache. We'll need to get to that as soon as we find Liz and make sure she's well. Cursed One? My *grathita* mentioned something about another Trueblood with Shadow marks."

Before Wyley could respond, a cry filled the night. A sound so terrifying that it stunned the large gathering into absolute silence. Again and again, the anguished screams traveled through the chilled night air.

"It's him." The Cursed One. It was his cry. And that could only mean one thing. Jasyn raced for the outer gate, Lux and Kit one step behind.

Kit took out his sword. "What's going on, Dydarren?"

He shouted over his shoulder, already knowing they were too late. "He's her mate...*grathita*. He must be. And I have a feeling no one told him about what happens during Trueblood Unity."

Lux looked like he might be ill. "No. Sylvain didn't tell me. We have to get to Liz. If she's had three doses of his blood... I can't believe she survived the first two. She's Unborn. Even a Trueblood can be sickened, sometimes to death from Shadow-cursed blood."

"Oh Goddess. Elizabeth."

"We'll find her, Nicolette. Don't worry."

Thank the Mother he hadn't given in to his desire to bite his own mate. That she hadn't had more than a taste of his blood. If he'd caused her any pain...

It didn't take Jasyn long to find him. At the base of a large tree Midnight rocked her limp body. He was murmuring to her, trying to wake her, no doubt completely unaware of the tears rolling down his cheeks.

"Sweet Mother protect us, it can't be." At Lux's whispered words the Wildman pushed the slumped body behind him, his fangs bared to the encroaching attackers. He barely looked human, and his eyes held not a trace of recognition.

"Careful, Lux. Remember how Zander reacted." Kit put his sword away slowly. He knew not to antagonize a Trueblood protecting his vulnerable *grathita* during the change. Regina had lay still as the dead for two days after the Mediator's third blood sharing and no one had been able to go near her for fear of sending Zander into a rage.

Jasyn was at a loss. He remembered what Liz had called him. "Midnight. Midnight, listen to me. You shared blood again, didn't you? With Liz. She's not dead, Midnight. She's not hurt."

The crazed vampire tilted his head, recognizing the name. Then he caught sight of the other men beside Jasyn and began his threatening growl again. Jasyn lowered his voice, never taking his eyes off the snarling man. "Lux, we may have a problem. Wildman was barely hanging on to his control *before* this happened. And he's stronger than most Truebloods I've seen. Including you." A Were transformation was painful, but it was nothing compared to the insane coma Truebloods experienced. Still, Jasyn thought about how he'd feel if strange men came upon Hannah when she was most vulnerable. He would kill the bastards.

"Kit, maybe we should go back—"

"Kit?" The voice was nearly indistinguishable. Midnight's piercing blue gaze honed in on the tall Sariel guard with deadly intent. If he recognized him as one of Liz's old lovers, there may be no way to avoid a confrontation.

Hannah's scent wafted over him, and Jasyn swore under his breath. "Let's just invite everyone to come and stare at him. That'll calm him down."

Hannah took a deep breath and stepped beyond the safety of the men, closer to Midnight. "Sleep!"

Nothing happened. His quiet growl intensified, and Jasyn's heart began to race. "Honey, step back. Slowly." His body tensed when instead of following his orders, she moved closer. If they got out of this intact, she was in for the spanking of her life.

Hannah's eyes were wide and unblinking. Wildman wove on his feet, but didn't collapse. Hannah wove with him, staring him down. His growling stopped, an expression of confusion crossing his features before he collapsed in a heap beside Liz.

"She's like a snake charmer. A beautiful snake charmer." Wyley, who'd obviously followed Hannah out into the woods, sounded impressed. Jasyn glared at the cowboy. Lux and Kit immediately went to the two unconscious bodies, Lux ensuring Liz was clothed before lifting her up in his arms.

He stopped beside Hannah, who looked a little shaken. "Glynn and Mysha said the connection between you and the children will continue to weaken. We need to do this now. This is far worse than anyone told me, and we only have a few hours before sunrise." She nodded and watched them walk back toward the Were compound, hugging herself as though she just realized she was cold.

Jasyn strode to her side and wrapped his arms around her, warming her with the heat from his body. He'd been a fool, thinking she couldn't handle everything he was. That she was too fragile to be his equal in every way.

"Yet another sin we share, Beta. She was born to our world with a broken heart. All I knew was I needed to protect her. From you. From pain. From everything. After all these years, that never changed. I didn't see she was capable of more."

"You scared me, honey. I was afraid your bravery might lose me my mate."

Hannah's wet laugh was muffled as she buried her face in his neck. "I'm not brave, Jasyn. Those kids are brave. Once their power is gone I'll be back to being just plain Hannah."

He lifted her chin to look into her stormy blue-grey eyes. "You've never been just plain anything, love. You're my Sheba. My mate. And as soon as this is over I'm going to spend the next eighty years showing you just how special you are." He rubbed a tear off her cheek and tried to smile. "Now what is it Lux wants you to do?"

She pulled away from him and starting walking back to the compound. "Nothing much. I think I have to go into Wildman's head and untangle the knots the Shadow's mark has made of his mind."

"What?"

"What?" Jasyn echoed Nicolette's voice in his mind. Anger at Lux for putting Hannah in that kind of position replaced every other emotion. He whipped Hannah around, stopping her from entering the compound.

She groaned. "I don't know why he's like that or who did it to him, but what I do know—and please Goddess don't ask me how I know this—is that those marks are a danger to Liz now too. Unity is too complete. Too intimate a joining. She'll be lost in his darkness, and there may not be a way to bring her back." She jerked out of his grasp. "We can't let that happen, Jasyn. If I can help, I'm going to."

"What can I do?"

Her shoulders drooped in relief, and she took his hand in hers. "Pray to the Goddess. That's all any of us can do right now. And cross your fingers that those kids knew what they were doing when they put their faith in me to save the day."

Chapter Six

"I just wanted you to know how sorry I am. I knew Alexei was capable of doing something like this, but I had no idea my twins would get involved as well. They obviously didn't think their parents were capable of handling the situation without their interference. You shouldn't have been put in the middle."

Hannah patted Lux's hand. "They were only trying to help. And believe me, they have. You have wonderful children, Lux. You and Arygon and Sylvain are very lucky."

He smiled through his worry, unable to completely hide his paternal pride. "They obviously take after their mother more than we thought. But this? That's all me I'm afraid." Hannah laughed softly, knowing it was true. Lux had always bucked the rules. Choosing to be a Healer instead of towing the political line of the Sariel family. Not one but two *grathitas*, male and female, and both werewolves. She didn't doubt that some of his rebelliousness rubbed off on his offspring.

Her smile faded when she looked down at the two bodies on the bed. Liz had been through so much, she deserved the happiness that came from Unity. But with him? He was barely civilized, borderline insane and an unrepentant killer. She'd watched the cold, emotionless way he'd torn the Shadow Wolves apart. She held no love for the Shadow, but Liz's *grathita* scared her. Why would the Goddess choose such a man?

She thought about Jasyn. Irritating, bossy, old-fashioned Were. Always underestimating her. Always keeping secrets. Yet, she loved him. She would die for him. Who was she to judge another's heart? "You reacted when you first saw him. Do you know him?"

Lux sobered as well. "I can hardly believe it myself, but I do. When Alexei first described the man he'd seen through your eyes, Sylvain told me Mysha almost fell over. He was a well-guarded secret of the Shadow. And someone my people believed to have died right before the Great War. Initially, I think he was the reason Malcolm joined the fight in the first place. And, like always, everyone followed Malcolm's lead."

"Liz's husband?"

"Her husband...and her *grathita's* twin brother. I was too young back then to fight or understand the turmoil going on around me, but I remember Malcolm weeping in my mother's arms over the disappearance and presumed death of his twin. Zander and I had always thought him invincible, seeing him so heartbroken was something I could never forget."

Kit, who'd been a silent shadow in the room, shook his head. "Too many secrets. And whoever's keeping them thinks they are important enough to destroy families, start wars and kill to keep. I just don't understand. Why this man? Why, if Nicolette and Jasyn were getting too close to the truth, wouldn't they just kill them and be done with it?"

Hannah sighed and looked back toward the bed. "Maybe he'll know. Lux, tell me what I need to do."

Lux joined her, all business. "I've forced a few of Glynn Magriel's concoctions down his throat, which should lower his guard enough to let us in. The most important thing you need to do is to get out of the way." Her confusion must have shown on her face. "The old women believe that they can help through

Alexei's connection to you. Think of yourself as a conduit. Clear your mind and let the knowledge flow through you."

"Is she in any danger?" Jasyn was leaning against the wall beside Kit, trying to appear calm, but she knew him better. He didn't like feeling helpless. Didn't like the idea that she would be facing an enemy that he couldn't see, couldn't fight.

Lux had no sympathy. "I won't lie. The first time I had to deal with marks like these were Regina's. They were nothing compared to these, and it took all my knowledge, and Zander's blood to heal her. I have never seen anything this complicated." He ran a hand through his hair. "From what you've told me, it seems to block him from thinking coherently. It obviously stops him from remembering who he is, or he would have returned home. Plus his own blood twin couldn't sense that his brother was alive. Someone took his time with this spell. Wanted to ensure it would last for the rest of his life."

Hannah couldn't imagine that kind of darkness. To exist without any sense of self, in total isolation, seemed fate far worse than death. And this man had been like this since before the war with the Shadow Wolves. Her heart ached for him. Lux touched her shoulder. "Good. Compassion and a desire to heal are key components to healing. Let it flow through you. Let it guide you."

She sensed Jasyn behind her before he turned her to face him. Her eyes closed at the tender touch of his lips on hers. "Stay safe, Sheba." Her lashes lifted to watch him walk away, rejoining Kit. Two guardians watching over them.

Hannah sat in a small chair beside the bed, with Lux walking over to the opposite side, sitting next to Liz. Lux rolled up his sleeve. "Damn it all, Lizzy. You certainly never do anything small." He met Hannah's gaze. "I'm even more concerned about her. Sariel blood is strong, the purest of the

Truebloods, and it helped to save Regina, to strengthen her defenses and aid in healing." He sighed. "She's strong, but she was still an Unborn. An Unborn who drank the blood and had sex with a very sick man. The Shadow's spells are like a sickness. An illness focused on a single task. And Liz has taken his illness into her own body. If we heal him, she may survive, but it's still very dangerous. I'm going to give her some of my blood, to give her a fighting chance."

Lux told her to rest her hands on Midnight. One beneath his neck, the other along his collarbone. "Now close your eyes, and open your mind. They are there, waiting to help."

She could feel them. Priestess Magriel, Mysha—Sylvain's guardian and a healer herself—the children and even Regina and Sylvain, sending their energy and love to the broken Trueblood through her.

Her mouth opened, words she didn't understand leaving her lips. Her awareness followed the words into the body beneath her hands, into his mind. Chaos. Darkness. Pain. She wanted to scream out with the pain that was all around her.

A small hand slipped into hers, and she looked down. Alexei. His golden locks were a beacon of light in the darkness, and his touch separated her from the pain. He pointed into the blackness. "Look."

The sharp, swirling darkness had turned into rooms sealed with heavy metal doors. A blue stream of light was prying open the closest door. She instinctively knew that the light had been created by the Healers. Hannah watched as the door cracked open, peering inside.

"Malcolm, stop. If you keep using your powers you'll sink the whole bloody island." The two teenage boys laughed at the shrieking woman yelling through the thunderstorm. One of them

moved his hand and waves of fog streamed in, covering their escape as they ran from the manor.

"Would that I had a power like yours, brother. Malcolm the Storm Bringer."

Malcolm patted the boy who could have been his mirror image on the back, laughing as they collapsed beneath the nearest tree, the rain finally dying down. "I like that. It makes me sound like a sorcerer. I may wash all evidence away, but you keep all our secrets hidden. What shall we call you? Marcus...the Midnight Fog."

His name was Marcus. Marcus Abaddon. Hannah allowed that knowledge in, guiding the light to another locked door. She felt intrusive. She was seeing things that only he and his mate should share. But they couldn't share them until the blackness that bound him set them free.

Each time the spell rained down on her like shards of pointed glass she felt Alexei's hand, Lux taking her arm or Glynn Magriel's touch on her shoulder, taking away the hurt. And each time a new door opened she saw another piece of this lost man's life.

His mother had left after giving birth to Sari and Sebastian. Marcus had always believed it was because of him, until he'd found out she'd left because of his father's cruelty.

Marcus had a thing for redheads. Malcolm teased him, called them his only weakness.

"You should train with me, not run after Bridget."

"She's running after me. I may even allow her to catch me."

"Rogue. Careful, lest Sebastian sees you. He would like nothing better than to tell tales to father."

"There is nothing I can do to please our sire. So I must do my best to displease him as well as I can."

The next image showed a more adult Marcus, his gaze cynical as he sat in a smoke filled den surrounded by female blood donors. He let people think he was a good for nothing playboy, a Trueblood who hated Trueblood rules. The opposite of his perfect twin brother. It made it easier to catch people off guard. Find out their secrets. And among his kind, there were so many.

He'd started to pull away from Malcolm, the brother he loved more than his own life. He couldn't share his suspicions with his twin, no matter how much he wanted to. Suspicions that his father was a part of something dark and twisted. That he had dealings with…even *he* had a hard time thinking it, and he hated the bastard.

This was the only way.

"Damn you, Marcus, is this what your life has become? A blood glutton, a bedtime story used to frighten children? We used to laugh at those men. This is not what The Mother—"

"If you mention your moon goddess to me again I shall become ill, brother Mal. I may be the glutton you name me to be, but what are you? A fop. All rules and no fangs. Where is the Storm Bringer that I used to know and admire?"

"I'm still here, brother. I always will be. Loving you and wishing you would come to your senses."

Another scene. An Elder approached him to come to a special gathering. Hannah could feel Marcus's excitement as the hooded figure gestured to him. This was the entry he'd been seeking. He would finally have answers. When he had proof he would go to Malcolm, repair the damage and reunite with his beloved brother and regain the respect of The Mediator,

Alexander, who'd been more like a father to him and Mal than their own.

Dark shafts of pain stabbed Hannah's head before she could see the other man's face. She fell to the ground, only this time there was no hand in hers, no touch to lift her out of the agony. A cold heavy weight filled her limbs, making her weak, tired.

This was what Liz felt before she lost consciousness. Hannah could see it clearly in his mind. She saw through his eyes as he caught her body when it fell from its perch high in the tree. He'd done this to her. The only light in his dark existence. He couldn't hear her thoughts, couldn't hear the questions she was constantly asking herself. He wanted those questions. He would gladly take the pain if only she would stay with him.

"Stay. Stay, wildcat. Don't leave me alone."

"Stay. Stay with me. Don't leave me alone." Strong arms lifted her out of her chair. Tears streamed down Hannah's face as she came back to herself. Jasyn. She buried her face in his neck, smelling the warm, earthy scent of him. Alive. Hers.

The soft voices behind her were jarring. "We undid the spell's center. His marks will fade over the next few risings, and as they do, everything that he is...that he knows, will return to him." Lux sounded as tired as she felt. "More importantly, he can think again. Question. And Liz will be safe."

"I'm taking Hannah to bed. Will she be all right?" Jasyn held her closer in response to her wiggling. She wanted to get closer. Needed to be with him. After all that darkness, she needed her mate.

"A few of his memories may linger. In order to clear the way for the others, she went further under than I thought she would. She did an amazing job really. Go. Kit will keep watch and I'll stay close, but he won't wake anytime soon. When he does he'll have a lot on his plate, poor bastard."

Her body lifted with the breath Jasyn took. "And you, Lux? My brother would use me to sharpen his claws if I left his mate looking the way you do now. Do you need anything? Food? Blood?"

Lux's chuckle was warm. "I'll be fine, brother. The sun is nearly on the horizon. Take her."

She still hadn't come out of the daze she'd fallen into since they'd left the others. Jasyn had put her beneath the heated shower spray, washing her with gentle but efficient hands. It was torture, trying not to think about what they'd been doing the last time they'd been here together. He dried her off and carried her to the bed. Blessing his American cousins for their thoughtfulness, he closed the seamless wooden blinds to block the sun before stripping off his clothes and climbing in beside her, to offer whatever comfort he could.

He thought about his brother Arygon's mate Sylvain. The *Antara*. A female Shadow who'd been forced to hide for most of her life because of her abilities to control the earth and all that grew in and on it. Weres believed the *Antara* was a sign of the end of everything. A mythical figure that, if she even existed, must be killed lest she use her powers to destroy.

She'd done the exact opposite, reminding werewolf and vampire alike of the Mother's presence in their lives. Of their true purpose. She helped bring the Weres together under her Alpha mate. She'd made a believer out of Jasyn, whose faith had been tested over the years. But her abilities still made her a target.

He did not envy Lux or Arygon having her for their mate. He loved her like the sister she was, and he adored his niece and nephew. Still, he knew that with Sylvain for a wife, his brother's worries would never end. He would live in fear that her light would be taken from him.

He had a taste of that tonight, when Hannah was trapped in the darkness of the Wildman's mind. Her temporary abilities made her special to others in a way that put her in danger. As he held her it hit him that it wouldn't matter what she was or what she could do. If he'd made her his when she was human, and all she had become was a Were, his mate, she would still be special to him. He would still need to protect her.

"Zander must feel the same about Regina. And now Alexei. But we always worry about losing the ones we love, don't we? Think we can't survive without them. We can...we just don't want to."

Nicolette was trying to help, he knew. But there was no doubt in his mind that Hannah was necessary for his survival. How he'd lasted so long without her, how he'd stayed away, was a mystery to him. But he couldn't leave her now. Even if she wanted him to go.

"Don't go. Stay with me." For a moment he thought she might be reliving the Trueblood's memories, but when he looked down she was gazing up at him with clear longing in her eyes. A need that matched his own.

He laid a gentle kiss on her forehead, evading her seeking lips. Her kisses drove him crazy, and he wanted to please her, before he lost himself to his animal's need to mate. He pressed his lips against her eyelids, her cheeks.

By the time his open mouth caressed the curve of her stomach she was moaning his name. Her scent grew stronger and he inhaled deeply. She was intoxicating. His Hannah. His

Sheba. He pushed back the covers and knelt between her legs.

"*Jasyn.*"

He spread her legs, hands gripping her thighs. Great Mother she was beautiful here. Pale curls that had turned to dark gold with her need, the lips of her pussy flushed for him. And the smell of her. Strong and sweet, like honey warmed in the sun. He had to taste her.

His blood pounded in his veins, filling his already stiff erection to the point of pain. His grip on her thighs tightened until her hips were off the bed, her soaked sex a breath away from his hungry mouth.

His gums ached, and his muscles stretched with the need to bury himself within her. To claim her as no one else ever had. And just like that his jealousy surfaced. "Such a pretty view. Who else has seen this hot pussy, my passionate Sheba? When we first met there'd been no one, I felt the proof of your innocence with my fingers. Despite your worldly claims, I knew you'd never felt pleasure until I gave it to you." He held her fast when she jumped in surprise. "I have to know, Hannah. I let you go, left you alone all these years, and I have to know. Who will I need to make you forget?"

For a moment she looked as though she might fight him, might push him away at his offensive question. Why did he have to do it? Ruin the moment when he had her here in his arms? His father had told him once that Weres who could not, or would not claim their mates suffered from jealous rages. The animal in him cried out to bite her, mark her. The man in him knew there was no excuse.

"*Men are idiots. I tell her so all the time. Egotistical idiots and hypocrites. You can sleep with any human, Were or vampire that comes your way. She has to stay locked in a tower pining for you. That's so eighteen hundreds of you, darling.*"

"Is it too much to ask for more privacy and less backseat driving?"

Hannah's hand touched his on her leg, and he met her gaze, ready to apologize. Grovel if necessary. It didn't matter. Nothing did now that they were together. But instead of censure, understanding shaped her expression, filling him with gratitude and, he had to admit, confusion. But he wasn't about to question his good fortune.

"No one, Jasyn. No one but you."

"All that time? Then, honey, we have a lot of catching up to do." He couldn't control the growl rumbling in his throat at the first taste of her on his tongue. Pure Hannah. His. He tugged her pussy lips with his teeth, the flat of his tongue gathering every drop of her arousal.

"Jasyn. Oh, yes Jasyn, *please.*" He felt Hannah's hands slide into his hair, but instead of pulling him away, she pressed him closer. He pushed forward until her knees were flush against her breasts, her hips high as he continued to lick and suck every inch of her sweet pussy.

No other woman had this effect on him. He couldn't stop, couldn't get enough of her honeyed juices. He spread her pussy lips wide with his fingers so he could get deeper, taste more. Her shout of approval when he thrust his tongue deep inside her made his cock jerk. He needed to make her come. Had to feel her pussy tighten around his tongue, swallow every drop of her climax down his throat.

His tongue curled inside her, pressing against the spot that made her scream, made her shudder against him. Her palms blazed against his temples, nails digging into his scalp. Beneath his lashes he watched as she turned her head, burying her face in the pillow to moan incoherently.

More. More. He pumped his tongue inside her, fucking her

with his mouth the way he wanted to with his cock. Hard and fast, deep as he could go. When his thumb pressed against her clit, he felt it. Her muscles clenched around his tongue, hands gripping his head so hard it should hurt, but all he felt was elation. The taste of her climax alone sent him close enough to touch the edge. He pressed the damp tip of his cock against her back to relieve the pressure as he continued to feast.

"Beta, something's—Dydarren!"

Jasyn's head was throbbing, satisfaction blindsided by a brilliant flash that made him feel as though his eyes were on fire. He rolled off the bed, away from Hannah, his hands covering his face protectively.

"Jasyn. Jasyn, talk to me. What is it? Hold on, baby, hold on. I'll go get Lux." He reached out with his eyes closed and gripped her ankle as she tried to get to the door. She landed on her knees beside him, cradling his head in her hands. "What have I done? I saw the light and I just…just…I'm sorry. Talk to me, please."

"Shh, Sheba." He nuzzled her belly with his lips, the need to soothe her overriding the pain. A pain that was fading with every deep breath. As his mind unscrambled he sensed that something was different. Something had changed. "Nicolette…she's gone."

"Gone? What do you mean gone?"

Hannah's voice rose with every word, and Jasyn winced. "She isn't here." His hand flew to his temple, and he struggled to sit up. "Hannah, is it still there? The mark? Is it gone?" She didn't answer, looking at him oddly as he wobbled to the bathroom mirror. He could still see the outline, but the tattoo-like mark was broken in spots, faded in others. "Hannah it's healing. It's healing, and Nicolette is—"

"She's safe. My connection to Alexei and the twins is getting weaker, but I do know she's safe, and we're not. We have to get back to England, back to Zander before the Shadow Wolves attack the compound and put all these innocents in danger."

Hannah stood and looked for the T-shirt and jeans Amy had found for her to wear. She kept her back turned to him so he wouldn't see her face. A moment ago she was flying, soaring at the feel of his mouth on her sex, bringing her to the heights of ecstasy. Now she was just trying not to cry.

She'd felt it, the power flowing through her, the ribbon of light as her moans of joy became a small chorus of healing voices flowing through her into him. If he'd taken whatever was in those vials Lux was carrying around, she was sure there would be no mark on him at all.

Her desire to heal him, to love him must have gotten through, calling the others whose minds she'd connected with only hours before. How could she allow herself to be angry that they'd used her orgasmic distraction to heal Jasyn and send Nicolette's consciousness back where it belonged? Her embarrassment was nothing when she thought about all those two had gone through. All Marcus Abaddon had suffered. So why was she upset?

"Great Mother the silence. The blessed silence. No lectures on the evils of men, no crude remarks about the fit of Wyley's jeans. Just man thoughts. Easy, uncomplicated, singular. I mean I'm glad she's safe, don't get me wrong...Hannah?"

She rubbed her wet cheeks on her shoulder as she slipped into a pair of clean cotton panties. "That's wonderful, Jasyn. I'm going to go check on Lux and the others, see when he thinks our patients will be ready to travel."

"The sun is up, you can't go out there. What the hell is the matter with you?" He spun her around, and it was all she could do not to burst into tears at his frustrated expression. She turned her head. "Look at me, Hannah. Five seconds ago you were screaming my name with your legs over my shoulders and my face between your thighs, now you can't even look at me?"

The vulgar words brought her gaze back to his. "Just let me go, Dydarren. You're free. No more Nicolette in your head. We're both back to where we started. And I need to get back to where I belong."

His hands gentled on her shoulders, caressing her soothingly. "You *are* where you belong, Sheba. With me." He pulled her closer, and she inhaled on a shaky sob. "What's this about, Hannah? What's going on inside your head?"

"I think I'm losing the connection. My abilities. *Their* abilities. I'm just me again." And how selfish was she for worrying about that now? But all she could think of was that she was a liability, a hindrance to them now. A fragile Unborn.

And Jasyn. Would their relationship go back to the way it had been before? With him believing, rightfully, that she was too fragile to be at his side?

Jasyn held her in silence. His heart, beating hard against her ear, was the only indication of his mood. That and the erection lengthening against her bare belly. A shiver of feminine knowledge ran through her at his body's reaction. A reminder that he'd been moments away from taking her, before the Shadow's mark had finally broken. Was she going to let her insecurity stand in the way of the kind of passion they had together? After all the time they'd lost, all the years she'd waited, she had to take this chance. To be brave.

"Hannah?"

"Yes, Jasyn?"

"We're all alone."

"Seems that way."

"Are you going to take those panties off while I watch or am I going to have to rip them off of you?"

Hannah pulled back to look into his sparkling eyes. He was smiling. And suddenly she was too. "The second option sounds more up your alley."

His grin widened, and Hannah could see the glint of his fangs. "It does, doesn't it?" The sound of cloth shredding and his wicked laughter made her blood sizzle. She turned toward the bed but he had other plans, making her dizzy as he spun her around and bent her over the arm of the quilt-covered recliner in the corner.

"I'm not waiting anymore, Sheba." He spread her legs with one of his own, an arm wrapped around her torso, his hand cupping her breast. His other gliding over her hip to slide between her thighs. "I wanted to give you time. Wanted to give you moonlight and yellow roses. But there is no perfect time or place. There's only now. The truth that you belong to me will never change. And you aren't leaving this room until you're finally mine in truth, marked and mated. I know it's not the romantic proposal you pictured. It's messy and dirty and raw. But it's real."

Hannah bit her lip, her hands braced on the springy chair, thinking she'd never heard of anything more wonderful in her entire life. All her insecurities and past hurts faded away. He was hers. The man she'd fallen for the instant she'd laid eyes on him. The Were she'd tried to hate, but always dreamt of. She wiggled her bottom against his erection, flipping her short blonde hair out of her eyes to throw him a saucy wink. "I love you too."

His eyes twinkled, glowing with an unnatural, beautiful light. She gasped at the first slow thrust of his cock inside her. Her sex stretched for him, clung to his flesh as he pulled his hips back just as languidly. She rose onto her toes with a cry when his hips met hers. So deep. And so slow it was torture. But Jasyn was taking his time, reveling in his claiming, holding her so tightly she couldn't force him to quicken his pace.

Over and over with total control and deliberation he fucked her. Her body was on fire, limbs trembling so hard she could barely hold herself up. "Jasyn, please."

"Say it again."

Say what again? She couldn't concentrate. She needed...something. Needed his bite. Needed more. *"Please."*

"Tell me you love me, Sheba. Tell me you love me, and I'll give you what you want."

"I love you. I love you. I, *ah—yes."* She threw her head back and cried out his name as he changed his rhythm, the chair shaking beneath her with the power of his thrusts. She clawed at the fabric of the chair, loving the wildness, loving him.

His body bowed over hers, and his steamy breath against her neck gave her a thrill of excitement. Yes. Now. Finally. A sharp, momentary pain and then he was there. With his fangs clamped down on her shoulder, his hands all over her body, and his cock deep inside her, Hannah wanted to howl for joy. She wanted to bite him in return. Taste him as he was tasting her.

"Your wish is my command." His hand left her breast and she nuzzled his wrist, piercing his flesh and moaning as his blood slid down her throat.

They came together in such an explosive conflagration that Hannah was sure she smelled smoke. They rocked together, both shaken, neither willing to separate from the other. She never wanted to be separated from him again.

"Never, Mate. My mate. Love you."

And she knew it was the truth. His feelings washed over her. His heart and mind were filled with memories. Snapshots of her.

The day he'd first seen her, sunlight in her hair, sketchpad in hand.

Watching her draw him while she thought he was sleeping, wanting her so badly he thought he might explode, or shift on the spot and send her running home to California.

After her accident. Walking for days, not knowing where he was going, or if he could bear to come back. Still loving her. Always loving her.

"Always, Sheba. Never doubt it."

She never would again.

Chapter Seven

"Good place to think. I climbed up here all the time as a pup. 'Course, when I came down again I'd get my ass tanned seven ways to Sunday."

"Planning on tanning my ass?" Midnight didn't have to look at Wyley to know he had paused before sitting beside him on the high compound wall.

"I'm not a fool. And I would never hurt someone who's been so important to my people." Wyley looked out into the twilight. "You were sleeping for two days, but those marks on your neck are really fading now. The big guy told me that they kept you from remembering who you were, and where you belonged. Will you leave the mountain now that you know?"

"I have no choice." His life was coming back to him like an ocean tide. There were large chunks that he still didn't recall, but he knew it was only a matter of time. That wasn't why he had to leave. "My *grathita* has run from me."

He knew why. Her rising after Unity couldn't have been easy on her. The truth of who he was had been a lot for her to take in. Especially since no one had ever told her he existed. Malcolm had never told her.

His brother had forgotten him, along with everyone else.

"*Grath*-oh you mean your mate. Amy told me she'd seen Liz tearing out of here like those Shadows were on her heels as soon as the sun went down. Never had a mate, but from what I've seen, they are exactly the sort of trouble I'd like to avoid. To tell you the truth, I'm surprised you aren't already on her trail."

He liked Wyley. There was no scent of fear on the Were, though he knew what Midnight could do to him. What he would have done to him only a few days before for mentioning Lizbeth. "She's safe. Overwhelmed with her new situation, but safe. She's on her way back to England. She needed time, so she has time." Long enough to arrive a few hours ahead of him. That was all the time away from her he was willing to spare.

"Big of you."

"Couldn't resist, could you, wildcat? But don't blame me for my desire to touch my *grathita*. *Just because I understand your reasons doesn't mean I have to like them.*"

He smiled at her stubborn silence. He didn't mind, he could feel her inside him with every breath he took. When he was younger, the idea of Unity was appalling. His father had tortured his mother with their connection, using it to manipulate her, to bend her to his will. A memory formed in his mind. Alexander Sariel had tried to convince him that cases like those were rare, that the Mother didn't make those kinds of mistakes, and usually finding and loving your *grathita* was the greatest gift a Trueblood could receive. It had been hard for him to believe. He believed now.

She was sex incarnate, long thick curls of flame, brilliant emerald eyes and a lean, feline body he knew he'd never have enough time on this Earth to explore. No fragile flower, his Lizbeth. She needed no one to fight her battles. She was, in a word, magnificent. And, even when he had been trapped in the Shadow's spell, he knew he needed her.

Night had fully descended once more, not that it mattered. He was old enough that his blood would protect Lizbeth from the light of the sun, and the Were who'd brought Liz to him had mated his own Unborn. Hannah's transformation would be swift. If they needed to fight, her initial transformation would be painful in comparison to a Trueblood shift. But Jasyn Dydarren would have to protect her. Midnight couldn't wait any longer. It was time to gather the others and go home. Luckily they would have a Healer on the journey.

Lux Sariel. Alexander's youngest son, all grown up and mated, and with twins of his own. It was hard for Midnight to reconcile all he'd missed. At times it seemed as though he'd just fallen asleep for a moment. He might believe it if he didn't recall every minute he had dwelt in his own personal purgatory as well. If only he could remember the Trueblood responsible. So he would know who to kill.

He leapt off the wall and strode back to the adobe apartments that held the others. Wyley landed on the ground beside him, trying to keep up. "If you're going, I was wondering if I could come along. Jasyn promised to introduce me to the European Alpha, and the more I hear about those Shadow Wolves, the more I think my claws could be put to better use than they would around here."

Midnight shrugged. "It's up to you. Are you the Alpha of your people?"

Wyley shrugged. "My people never really cottoned to that kind of power structure. They came here to get away from the rules and ingrained instincts that shaped them. But I do most of the trading in town, and break up the scuffles during mating season. I guess I'm as close to an Alpha as we have. But don't underestimate Amy. That female is tough as nails if you get out of line."

His smile was disarming, but Midnight had a feeling the Were's western charm was not entirely genuine. He was too wary of the Cursed One. Still, he'd never sensed any malice from these Weres. In fact, in a way they'd been a comfort to him all these years. He nodded. "Come. But do not underestimate the Shadow's abilities. They are not as vulnerable as they seem."

He rubbed his neck, knowing the marks were still there, but fading rapidly. The Shadow Wolves. Lizbeth's belief that they were extinct was false, he knew. Her experiences with the psychotic Grey Wolf and Gyvain, both dead, had led her to believe that the others had scattered to the winds. He knew better. They may not be around in the numbers they'd had before, but there were enough to cause significant damage.

Look at what a single Shadow had accomplished. Grey Wolf had taken Sebastian's weakness and used it toward his own ends. They'd killed Malcolm and made it look like a random Were attack. Not Shadow. Not the purpose driven murder it was. He felt no sorrow for Sebastian's death. His younger brother had finally gotten what he wanted when he became the heir of the Elder Abaddon. Midnight's only regret was that he hadn't been the one to kill his power hungry younger brother.

"Well, that settles it. I'm coming with you. But I can't go around calling you Cursed One all the time. It seems rude now that we've bonded. Would you mind if I called you Marcus?"

"Midnight. My name is Midnight." He couldn't think of himself as Marcus Abaddon. That naïve Trueblood had allowed hundreds of years, his family, his entire life to be stolen right out from under him.

Marcus was dead. Long live Midnight Fog.

The headache was finally gone. Liz felt normal again. As normal as she could under the circumstances. It didn't make any sense. None of it. Why wouldn't Malcolm have told her he had another brother? A *twin*? Liz thought of all the opportunities he'd had from the moment he'd first introduced her to Sebastian and Sari, to the evening she'd woke to find him dead in the kitchen. They'd shared everything. There was no being, human or other, on the planet who'd known more about her.

"Until now."

She ignored Midnight's intrusion, but knew he was right. Regina hadn't been exaggerating. Not just about the heightened senses, but about the connection as well. She'd created Unborns, shared blood with lovers, with her husband Malcolm, himself a Trueblood, but it had never been like this. This intimate. This complete.

He knew how she'd struggled after her father had put her out with only the clothes on her back. The nights of hunger. The things she'd done for a warm place to sleep. For a plate of food.

She'd made her way to London, looking for a new life, but it had been harder than she'd thought. No one had cared. No one had seen her. Except for the filthy men with rotting teeth and jangling pockets who had wanted a quick toss in the corner.

The irony of her fate wasn't lost on her. She'd been innocent of the accusations her father had laid at her feet. She'd been a good girl, stubborn and more opinionated than most, but still a good girl. Then, because she'd been left with no choice, she'd become the whore he'd always imagined she was. She could never go back home.

Her life had stretched out before her. Too short, filled with pain and humiliation and an early grave. Until one unbearably cold night, yet another spent on the dark, stench filled streets that she'd seen him.

Her first vampire.

Long hair so blond it had seemed white in the moonlight. Tall and broad shouldered with smooth, glowing skin unmarred by pox or scar. His glinting amber gaze that had trained on her when she rounded the corner the instant before he had bitten into the throat of another working woman, moaning at the taste of her blood.

He'd had fangs. Sharp, white fangs that had slid into the woman's rough flesh as though it were cream. She had watched as his other hand disappeared beneath the whore's skirts, his arm pumping in time to her sounds of pleasure. Pleasure?

She'd heard of creatures like this. Monsters that hid behind a beautiful façade. Demons who seduced you, beguiled you with their soft words and irresistible touch. Who only killed when their victims had reached the heights of satisfaction.

They were stories told to children to scare them into staying close to home. But Elizabeth had been more fascinated than afraid. The power rolling off him had been seductive. Would that she had that power. Over life. Over death itself. She would never have to suffer again.

When the body in his embrace had gone limp, he'd dropped it to the cobbled streets without sparing it a glance. As he had strode toward her, blood dripping down his chin, she'd realized for the first time that she was in jeopardy. He had been coming for her. For a moment she had been tempted to let him take her. To feel pleasure in her final moments. To feel something other than cold and hunger.

Her instinct to survive had reared its head at the last moment, and she'd turned to run, only to find her way blocked by a pair of strong arms.

"She isn't for you. Clean up your mess before I take up your new hobby with the Clan Trust. And never let me catch you harming an innocent again."

"An innocent? What, Malcolm? Have you taken to roaming the streets like some avenging angel? The war is over my friend. Life is sweet. You have all the others bowing and scraping, but do not pretend heroics with me. We both know you're partial to redheads." The creature had laughed. "Must run in the family."

Elizabeth had heard him walk away, her heart pounding in her throat. Was this another then? She took a fortifying breath, lifting her chin to face her savior, or her end, as bravely as she could.

Angel indeed. The most beautiful man she'd ever seen. Dark hair and long lashed eyes swirling with unusual blue and purple hues. He'd studied her intently, as though looking for some answer in her eyes. And then he'd smiled. "You're safe with me. Come, it's a cold night. Food and drink will warm you."

"Will'na ye bite me, then?"

His smile had grown at her thick accent. "Not tonight, lass. And when I do, it won't be like that." He had gestured to the pool of blood left behind on the ground. He'd wrapped one arm around her shoulder and led her to the nearest pub, finding a seat near the fire, and had ordered enough food to feed all five of her brothers.

She'd fallen a little in love with him that night. The man with the beautiful face and tender heart. He'd told her more than she ever wanted to know about vampires, werewolves and war. He never held back the truth from her, even when she didn't want to hear it. He'd married her and lived with her for a few, short, blissful years.

Liz came back to the present with a heavy heart. But he'd never told her about the brother he'd lost. The brother who was her true blood mate. Another Abaddon. The Mother was surely having a laugh at her expense. But she couldn't deny that the knowledge had hurt her, confused her on so many levels that she had to run. *Mal, you should have told me.*

Nothing. He was no longer the voice in her head. No longer her silent cheerleader. The last remnant of the man who'd saved her from the untenable life she would have led back then, a woman alone, was gone.

She felt her mate's sadness when he thought of Malcolm. The brother he'd been so close to, lost to him before he could tell him why he'd been so distant. Why he'd pulled away. She couldn't help but admire the sacrifices Midnight had made to protect his brother. The memories were murky, unclear, about how he was taken, and why. But the love he felt for Malcolm had shone through the darkness. Along with his feelings for her. His blood mate.

Not Unborn now but Trueblood. For so long Liz had defined herself as an outcast. The founder of the Deva Clan and hater of all things Trueblood. And then her Gypsy had joined with a Sariel, and Lux had come back into her life. The Priestess Glynn Magriel had lost sleep working to save Nicolette. All of them holding pieces of her heart. All of them Truebloods.

And now so was she.

She'd had to leave when she'd woken up beside the unconscious Midnight. Had to think. But most of all, she had to see Nicolette and discover why this had happened. What secret was so important that it had to be kept at this cost?

The pub was finally in view. Haven. She should have been here sooner, but she'd needed to think. The evening was in full swing inside. She could hear the music, the breathing of more than eighty beings, vampire and human. Their world had continued as it always had, even though hers had been irrevocably changed. She stopped for a moment in the alley, trying to slow her racing heart. She knew more, could feel more than she ever had before. The world was brighter, sounds intensified, and her instincts had never been sharper.

This morning she'd seen daylight. Through the tinted window of her plane and the sunglasses she'd never had the need for until today. Midnight was older than Zander or Lux, as old and powerful as Malcolm had been.

There were times Mal would leave their bed to watch the sunrise, watch the humans starting their world turning. He'd tell her that, apart from being with her, it was his favorite thing to do. The dawn *had* been beautiful. And strange. Luckily she'd landed and found shelter before the full heat of the day. But after all this time in the darkness, the light was breathtaking.

Gripping her knapsack in trembling hands, she headed toward the sign, red lion rampant and the words Ye Olde Haven Pub etched upon it. Liz took a deep breath and pushed open the doors.

The music was loud. Bodies writhing on the small dance floor while the crowded leather booths filled with whispered conversations. Conversations that began to lessen as Truebloods who recognized the Deva Clan leader looked her way. They could sense the difference in her, and she wasn't sure who was more shocked, her or them. In moments all gazes were turned her way, some smiling in malicious delight, others with eyebrows lifted to their hairline at this stunning turn of events. This was ridiculous.

She planted her hands on her hips and stared them all down. "Yes, yes, it's very exciting. Another Deva bites the dust. Pureness triumphs and all is right with the world. Gossip about it while I'm gone, there's a good group of bloodsuckers." She turned and plowed forward to the door leading up to the lofts above, Midnight's laughter ringing in her ears.

"*My woman.*"

He sounded proud of her. Not embarrassed by the scene she just made in front of the other Truebloods. She'd tried hard to keep her head down when she was with Malcolm, to be a good wife to him, but she knew the mere fact of her existence made life difficult for him with his people.

"I cannot speak for my brother, but why would I be embarrassed, wildcat? You are mine. My lover. My grathita. *I am the envy of all the bloodsuckers."* He chuckled again, using her word for the vampires muttering behind her. *"You are running out of time to prepare for me, my love. I've almost arrived."*

Shit. She tried to hide the thrill of excitement she felt at his words, tried to pretend she was aggravated by his domineering ways. But she missed him. Wanted his touch, wanted her wild man to take her the way he had before.

Their last encounter, when he'd taken her high up in the trees, had been electrifying. Animalistic. She'd never felt so alive. Even now, her body trembled at the memory, her sex tingling, readying itself for his cock, his mouth.

She thought about being restrained again, this time on her bed in Deva castle. Her wrists would be bound to the posts with silken scarves, her body his to do with as he would. She wanted to introduce him to her toys. To feel him filling her ass again as he fucked her pussy with her favorite vibrator. She wanted—

"That line of thinking is doing nothing to delay me, Lizbeth." The voice in her head was rough with his own renewed passion. She shivered, walking slowly up the stairs as he whispered in her mind *"I will give you all you want and more. Would you like to hear what I've been imagining? Wanting? I want to bend you over those stairs and kneel at your feet. Want to drink your sweet cream, lap every drop until I'm sated. Spread the soft cheeks of your ass and taste you there as well. Unbutton those tight leather pants, wildcat. Touch yourself for me."*

She couldn't resist. She was so aroused and she could sense no one on the stairwell, no one would know.

"No one but you and I. Do it, wildcat."

She slipped the top button out of its loop, then another, until her leathers were spread wide and loose. Her hand caressed her lower belly, hesitating.

"Don't tease me. Slide your fingers through those tight auburn curls and feel how wet you are for me. Show me how much you want me. Need me."

One hand gripped the railing as she obeyed, moaning at the wetness beneath her fingers, the wonderful pressure of her palm against her clit.

"Before now it's been wild and fast. Too fast. I want time to taste every inch of you. Make you come with my mouth, my hands, those toys of yours. And when I've made you come so many times you're sure you have nothing left, then I'm going to fuck you. Fill that hot pussy with my cock instead of your fingers. But now I want you to fuck yourself for me, wildcat. Three fingers, that's right. Deep. I want to fuck you deep."

She fell to her knees, pumping her fingers inside her sex, imagining they were his. His need fed off of hers, and she couldn't tell where his desires ended and hers began. But both were focused on making her come.

"Goddess, I wish I could watch you. Wish I could watch you riding your hand for me. Tell me, Lizbeth. Tell me who you belong to, who your grathita is."

"You are. I belong to you." Mother help her, it felt so good, but she needed more. She couldn't get deep enough. Couldn't thrust hard enough. She needed him. Needed to feel her mate.

"I'm close to you whenever you need me. Can you feel how close?" A naked male body was suddenly behind her, pressed against her, and she jerked in surprise. "Can you feel me now, wildcat?"

She'd been so caught up in her own need for pleasure that she hadn't sensed his arrival. Her pants disappeared and there was nothing between her heated skin and his. "Aye. Oh, aye."

"That's what I wanted to hear." He kissed her neck, one of his hands covering hers as she continued to thrust her hips against her hand. "As beautiful as this is, I'm jealous. I want to be the one inside you." He removed her fingers, licked them, and then placed her damp hand on the railing beside the other.

"Please. *Please.*"

"Please what, Lizbeth? Tell me what you want."

"You. I want you. Your cock deep inside me. Fuck me, mate. Wild and fast."

"Anything, grathita *mine."*

She bit her cheek hard to hold back her scream of need as the head of his cock pressed inside her. Slowly, teasingly. Every sensation was heightened by their new connection. His pleasure as her sex drenched him. She gripped the railing tight and pushed back against him until his hips were pressing into hers, every long, hard inch of him deep inside her.

"Fuck."

"Aye. Fuck me. Fuck me."

He growled, the only warning she had before her mate took over. So deep. He was fucking her so deep. This was what she needed. What she'd been dying for. Her wild man. Midnight.

He spread her cheeks and pressed his thumb against her ass. "Is this what you want, wildcat?" She inhaled sharply as he pushed inside, loving the feel of her muscles relaxing to take him. "You like being filled front and back?"

"Aye."

"I don't think I could share you, Lizbeth. Not in a thousand

years. But you'll never be sorry." He added another finger, her back arching at the delicious stretch. Again and again he took her to the edge, sharing through their connection all that he felt for her, how hard it was for him to hold back.

He hesitated before biting her. "I almost killed you."

She knew he was thinking about her illness. About what the Shadow's curse had nearly done to her and she shook her head. "You didn't. Don't stop, baby. Bite me."

He sank his fangs into her neck, and that was all it took. They came together, the world disappearing as they reveled in their shared climax. Unity. This was what it was. What it meant. A connection that nothing could sever, not even death.

Without warning, Malcolm's face appeared in her mind. His expression the moment he realized she wasn't his true mate. The sadness he couldn't quite hide. She'd never understood until now. When you knew something like this existed for you, anything less was, well, *less*.

Midnight's body, lax with satisfaction, tensed. Damn it. He pulled out of her body, clothing them both in an instant.

"*Someday other men won't fill your mind when I touch you.*"

"*Midnight, I'm sorry. I didn't mean to...*"

She started to turn to face him, but something stopped her. Large blue grey eyes, wide with shock. And arousal. Hannah stood, her mouth covered by Jasyn's hand. He was grinning. The beast. "You two have a little exhibitionism thing going on. I understand. I just wish you'd found a room, because I'm damned uncomfortable right now. Especially with Wyley and Lux here."

Liz caught the tip of a dusty cowboy hat and a flash of long, burgundy hair and closed her eyes. Just what she needed. An audience. She'd wanted time to explain. It was all happening so fast, and it was hard for her to come to grips with everything.

Her feelings were chaotic. Unbelievable and intense. But chaotic.

"You're mine, Lizbeth. I can see I just need to be more persuasive. Next time."

He helped her up, his hand wrapped possessively around her waist. "Now let's go see your friend, Nicolette."

They walked up the stairs, the others following. Liz couldn't be sorry that he was here with her. As much as she hated to admit it, she was beginning to need him. His strength. As if hers was somehow connected to his.

"Unity doesn't make you weak, wildcat. It adds to what you already are."

He caressed her hip with his fingers, and she nodded. She knew it was true, and yet, even with this connection, it was hard for her to let go of old habits. Hard to trust that something wasn't waiting around the corner to rip it all away.

They headed toward the room and her throat closed. The door to Nicolette's loft was ajar.

The room was empty.

Liz tried to push back her creeping concern. "Hannah? Have you tried to communicate with your sire?"

Hannah blushed. "I haven't thought about anything since..."

"The Were and Unborn have mated as well, Lizbeth. I'm sure that has affected the strength of her connection."

Liz sighed. "Can you try?"

Hannah tilted her head in concentration. "It's not as strong, but she's there. She says the Healers left, she spoke to the children for a while and then, after they'd nodded off, she decided to go and see Elder Abaddon." Hannah's forehead wrinkled. "She sounds...wonky. I don't know how else to describe it. She didn't even call me darling. Didn't ask me where I was, how you were. Nothing."

"Why the hell would she go back there without us?" Liz pushed past Jasyn and Wyley without apology and crossed the hall. She threw open the door to Zander and Regina's apartment. "I need to speak to Alexei."

"I told you we should've gone back to the estate. There's less interruption."

"Babe, I'd rather Liz walk in on us than your mother." Regina scrambled out of the bed, a robe covering her body before her feet hit the floor. "Although I wasn't expecting an entire entourage. I was worried, Liz. I'm glad you're back." She hugged her warmly while her golden gaze landed with delight on Midnight. "Zander has told me all he remembered about you, which isn't much. I've been dying to meet the Trueblood that finally...Liz? Liz what's wrong?"

"Where's Alexei? Pax? Rhys?"

Regina stepped back, and Zander came around the other side of the bed, his smiling gaze studying Midnight intently. "They are across the hall visiting with Nicolette. Alexei couldn't wait to see her once Mysha and Glynn pronounced her fit for visitors. And we were glad to have our favorite babysitter back for a moment." His laughter faded in the silence. "Elizabeth, is everything all right?"

"Nicolette left them in the loft and returned to Abaddon manor. But we've just been in the room." Liz saw a spark of panic light in Regina's eyes. "The children are missing."

Chapter Eight

Regina stumbled, would have fallen if Liz hadn't been there to catch her. "Haven is protected. How could anyone have gotten to them?"

Liz sensed the Reader reaching out, her mind scanning those below, reading Liz. "No one saw them. No one saw anyone come or go until Liz arrived."

Liz's head hurt from the panicked mother's mental searching. It was as though she couldn't stop, couldn't quite believe that no one had seen her child. That *she* hadn't sensed his cries for help.

"Reggie, you need to calm down. Pull back. You could hurt someone." Liz wrapped her arms around the petite beauty, holding her as she looked around the room. "Hannah, go check the room again, we may have missed something. Zander, you and Lux close the pub and talk to the Sariel guards. Where's Kit?"

Wyley stepped forward. "We, uh, parted ways when he went to pick up his wife. Said he thought the Cursed—I mean Midnight here might need some time to get used to him."

Liz met Midnight's unapologetic gaze. *"I am a 'wild man' remember? I do not share what is mine."*

"Oh for the love of—there's nothing between us."

"Not anymore."

Jasyn joined Hannah and Lux and Zander moved swiftly, needing to take action, needing to do something. Liz turned back toward Regina. "Just breathe, little Gypsy. I don't think someone took them. And you don't either."

Regina shook her head. "He wouldn't have. After the danger he and the twins put Hannah in, he promised... Why would Nicolette let him?"

"She wouldn't. Nicolette didn't know. She left them fast asleep. Safe."

Regina pulled out of Liz's embrace, using her abilities to dress herself in black jeans and a T-shirt with a thought. "Let's go. We need to find my son, so I can lock him in his room for the next century. And what the hell is Nicolette thinking, going back to that mad house?"

"We can both ask her as we drag her out by her hair."

"I feel like I'm intruding, but is there anything I can do?" Wyley looked decidedly uncomfortable, so different from the laid back Were Liz had met in Montana. No doubt being surrounded by so many vampires would make any werewolf a bit edgy. He caught her eye, and his cheeks darkened.

Jasyn pulled Hannah in behind him, smiling in understanding at the American Were. "You're fine, Wyley. You can distract Nicolette while we hog-tie her if you like. She has a little crush on you."

Wyley took off his hat and crushed it between his hands nervously. "She does? But I've never had the pleasure..."

Regina looked him up and down, distracted for a moment from her worry. "You will." She shifted on the balls of her feet. "Hannah, did you find anything?"

Without a word Hannah handed a crumpled note to Regina,

who read the childlike scrawl quickly, and then again, landing on the edge of the bed when her knees gave out.

Liz took the paper from her friend's limp hand. It was from Alexei. They should have named the child Houdini. He could block better than his mother ever could.

I'm sorry we left when you said not to. Don't worry I am watching the twins. Max is following Aunt Nicolette. We are following Max. She is still in danger until we find the secret. We will hide in the special place in her room until you come.

Luv,

Alexei, Pax & Rhys

"When we have children, remind me of this day, Lizbeth."

"Children?"

They'd all gathered downstairs. The Sariels, their guards—*sans* Max and Kit, and Sylvain. "I left the twins with Max and Nicolette to take Mysha to visit Glynn Magriel at her home. When Lux sent word to me, I went to the ruins, thinking they might be there." Lux hugged his mate close, his expression grim.

The ruins. The Sariel's underground safe house where Zander and Lux had taken Regina after Grey Wolf attacked Haven. But they all knew it wasn't where Alexei had gone. Alexei had taken children with Were blood into Abaddon manor. The adults in the room were all hoping the six-year-old had enough power left to block those of the Abaddon Clan who might use Pax and Rhys as an example.

Liz shook her head. "The special place? That manor is all smoke and mirrors, full of trap doors and secret hallways. But as far as I knew, there was nothing in Malcolm's room. Nothing where Nicolette was staying."

Lux and Zander turned toward Midnight, who was rubbing the back of his neck with a pained expression. "It's jumbled, memories out of time or unclear. But when I heard the words special place, I saw something. I think I could find it."

"Do we want anyone to know you're here yet?" Wyley took a step back when they all whipped around to stare at him. "It just strikes me that this secret might be connected to Midnight."

Zander Sariel strode up to the lanky Were and stared him down, every inch the intimidating Mediator. "Shadow Wolves marked him. Everyone, including his twin brother believed him dead. What makes *you* think his family wouldn't be overjoyed at his return?"

"Don't piss all over the boy, Zan. He's only saying what we already know." Midnight moved to stand beside Wyley in silent support.

Zander's lips quirked. "You and Malcolm used to call me Zan. I'd forgotten."

Midnight smiled. "So had I." He gestured to Wyley. "He's a smart Were. Alpha if I ever saw one. And he's right. There were marks from Shadow on my skin, but I was trapped by Truebloods. The information Nicolette and Jasyn found no doubt alluded to the same connection mine did." Jasyn nodded, and Midnight continued. "So the not so secret secret is revealed. A devil's bargain, formed before we were born, is responsible for the start of the war. Though it doesn't seem to have turned out the way they wanted."

"The way who wanted? What did they want? What the hell were you into, Marcus?" Regina stood closer to Zander, comforting him.

Liz had the desire to do the same for Midnight, but he shook his head, not taking his gaze from the Sariel. "The *asura saMsaki*, the Demon Coalition."

"That's just a conspiracy theory of bored vampires."

Midnight shook his head at Zander's flippancy. "They wanted anarchy and chaos, a world without Trueblood or Were law, where only the strongest Clan survived and the humans were naught but cattle."

Regina touched the bindu mark on her forehead. "The way it was before the Mother created Readers to maintain the balance."

Midnight dipped his head. "Exactly. And despite your arrival, and the death of the known Shadow leaders, it seems some of the members are still hard at work, determined to keep their secrets buried."

Lux narrowed his brilliant blue eyes. "Who? Name names, Midnight, that we might repay them for all the Trueblood slaughtered during the war."

"I don't know. I'm not sure if I never did, or I just don't remember yet. But there was an Elder I was highly suspicious of."

"Who?"

"Elder Abaddon. My father."

Wyley, Jasyn and Hannah were assigned to stay behind, in case Max or the children returned. The fact that they were Weres no doubt had something to do with it. Sylvain was the exception. There was no keeping the mother from joining the others. As *Antara*, Jasyn supposed she had that right. What would they do? Turn away a woman who could rend their house in two with a few well-placed quakes?

He wanted to be there. A Were was wired to protect their own. His niece, his nephew. Even Nicolette. After their forced intimacy he had to admit his feelings for her had changed. He cared about her and wanted her to find happiness. Someone to love her. He'd sensed her loneliness when he'd taken Hannah. The deep ache inside her for passion and companionship. Jasyn would storm that manor and help her if he could, keep her safe.

He could only imagine how his brother Arygon must be feeling, so far away from his mates with his children in danger. Jasyn would be climbing the walls. Or tearing them down to get to his kids.

He hadn't let himself think of children for so long. But the only woman he'd ever imagined as their mother was finally his. At last. His mate. Hannah. He studied her, curled up in the corner by the fire. Her eyes were closed in concentration. She was searching for any thread, no matter how slender, of the connection she'd shared with Alexei and the twins since Nicolette was purposely ignoring her. Desperate to help in any way she could, and just as unhappy as he was at being left behind.

But she was Were now. Though she hadn't shifted yet, her genetic makeup was changing. Her scent was changing. Still Hannah, but richer, fuller. Were. He wanted the taste of her on his tongue again. Wanted to lay her across the bed, down on the floor, and please her until she was howling with her release.

"You're distracting me."

"You're distracting me, Sheba."

His nostrils flared, instincts suddenly on alert. Wyley was staring at Hannah as well, his expression far from innocent. He was surprised that he felt no jealousy. Wyley was a good Were, and Jasyn couldn't help but like him. He also knew Wyley was responsible for the others coming to help them fight the Shadow Wolves. He respected him. An idea began to form in his mind.

"You're distracting our cowboy as well."

"Wyley?" She took a breath, biting her lip as she tested out her enhanced sense of smell. *"I'm sure he doesn't mean anything by it, Jasyn. You're both just hitting on all sixes after that floor show Liz and Midnight put on earlier, and angry at being left out of the rescue."*

"Hitting on all sixes?"

"Revved up. You know what I mean."

"I just love to tease you, mate. You may be right. But you'd be lying if you said you weren't feeling the same."

Jasyn got to his feet, drawing the American's gaze. "Wyley. Did you know that my brother's sexual preferences are unique for Weres in this part of the world?"

Wyley, who'd taken off his hat when they'd settled into the room, scratched his head at the unusual question. "I'll admit it's not the norm where I'm from, but it isn't entirely unique either. No Were I've met ever had *two* mates though. I don't know whether to admire him or feel sorry for him."

"Admire him." Hannah's expression was priceless when she realized that the words had escaped her lips. Her lush bow mouth formed a perfect O of surprise, and her cheeks flushed a delightful shade of crimson.

Jasyn smiled, and she narrowed her gaze.

"I used to believe as my father did, that Arygon's difference would only bring him heartache. Shame the Dydarren Pack. I was a fool about so many things. But I've changed."

"What are you up to, Jasyn?"

Wyley was looking at him with an odd expression. Jasyn chuckled. The poor Were was no doubt wondering where this was going as well. Adrenaline pumped through his veins. Maybe it *was* the frustration of inaction, the arousal that came from watching the rough love play on the stairs. Or the fact that being mated to Hannah made him feel more secure in their love, in himself, than he'd ever been before.

"My brother told me once that nothing could compare to the joy of being able to pleasure your mate thoroughly, to sate her completely, directing her pleasure and fulfilling all her fantasies."

"You wouldn't."

"Making Hannah my mate made my all of my fantasies come true. Joining with her soul and mind has made me a better Were, a better man, and I realized my brother was right. Nothing is more important than her pleasure." Her suspicious expression didn't change, but he felt her heart flutter. He knew she felt the same. "It also gave me a few interesting insights into *her* fantasies. One in particular, one she's had since my brother brought his mates back to Dydarren land, interests me most of all."

"Don't you dare."

A smile pulled at the corners of Wyley's mouth. "I'm not sure she appreciates you sharing that, though I'm certainly enjoying it."

Jasyn came to sit beside Hannah. She was glaring at him, but the aroma of her arousal filled the room. Wyley shifted on the couch across from her, looking for Jasyn to continue. "Weres are a passionate species, Sheba. I know you're feeling it now. You can't hide it from me."

"Is this a test? You've always been jealous, Jasyn. And for future reference, I would kill you for telling me you wanted to be with another woman."

"You are more than enough woman to last me a lifetime, my love. But this is no test. Search my heart. You know it's true. If you tell me you aren't the slightest bit tempted, just this once, to experience two men caressing you, tasting you, I'll send Wyley *away and make love to my mate."*

He felt her in his mind. Saw her glance over at Wyley and blush. The Were leaned back, crossing his arms over his chest as though he hadn't a care in the world. The erection pressing against his jeans belied his casual demeanor. "I feel like I'm missing an interesting conversation."

Jasyn wrapped his arm over Hannah's shoulder, his fingers caressing the curve of her breast. "Isn't she beautiful? The first time I saw her, I thought the Goddess herself had fashioned her just for me."

"You are a lucky man, Dydarren."

Hannah shook her head. "This is hardly the time for games, guys. We should be—"

"What? Pacing the loft like caged animals? Wouldn't you rather come sit on my lap and show Wyley why I can't get enough of my mate?" Jasyn felt like shouting in triumph when those perfect pearl white teeth bit into her lower lip once more. Tempted. She was willing. That was all the encouragement he needed.

He slid his other arm under her legs, until her jean-covered curves were pressed against his burgeoning erection. A part of him couldn't believe he was considering sharing her, that he would let another touch her this way. Kiss her. The animal inside him that demanded he claim his mate was the same one who pushed him to cup her breast through her cotton shirt, plucking at her nipple until it poked through the cloth.

Hannah's breath was shallow, her breast pushing into his hand despite her awareness of their audience. Jasyn sensed Wyley leaning forward, all pretense of disinterest gone. "I'm going to take off your shirt, Sheba. So Wyley can see your beautiful breasts."

She didn't say no, didn't say anything, just stared at him

with wide, fascinated eyes. Her arms lifted when he took the hem of her shirt in his hands, and he lifted it over her head, dropping the T-shirt on the floor behind the couch.

Wyley's sharp inhalation was telling. She was exquisite, and both men were riveted by the long, pink nipples, the flushed cream of her breasts, quivering with every breath, every heartbeat. Jasyn dipped his head to suck one hard tip into his mouth, circling the other with his rough fingertips.

Hannah moaned, arching her back. He could feel how sensitive she was there, exactly how she loved his touch. Her taste under his tongue made him burn, he needed more. He picked her up, unwilling to lift his head from her breast as he carried her to the bed. Her legs dangled off the bed as he unbuttoned her jeans and dragged them off her hips.

He lifted his mouth and stood between her thighs, taking off his own clothes. The look in her eyes as she studied his body was everything she could ask of a mate and more. She licked her lips, lifting up on her elbows to see all of him. "You see anything you like, Sheba? Anything you want?"

"You know I do."

Jasyn knelt at the foot of the bed, his mouth watering at the luscious scent of her arousal. "Wyley, why don't you join us? Hannah's breasts are just begging to be sucked."

He chuckled when her thigh muscles rippled against his shoulders. She'd been so lost in sensation she'd almost forgotten Wyley was there. Almost. "I'd love to give you what you need, baby, but I've been dreaming of this sweet pussy since we left Montana. I need another taste."

He licked her thigh slowly, watching Wyley, who'd removed his shirt, edge hesitantly toward the bed. Their eyes met, and Jasyn knew the other Were understood his boundaries. With Hannah, Jasyn was the Alpha, and Wyley would follow his lead in all things.

Hannah watched the lean man climb onto the bed beside her, his smile full of sensuality and admiration. "Your mate is right, Miss Hannah. You are beautiful." Her hands fell away from her body, giving him silent permission to touch. Jasyn's mouth moved closer to her sex, nibbling on the silken skin while Wyley caressed the inside of her arm and shoulder.

Jasyn couldn't wait any longer. He growled against her clit, and she cried out his name, lifting her hips closer to his mouth. "More. Jasyn. Oh!"

He opened his eyes, sensing her shock as Wyley lowered his mouth to her breast. He stilled for a moment, searching her mind to ensure it was pleasure she was feeling. She was surprised for a moment, but the feel of two mouths on her body was erotic, intoxicating. Wyley closed his teeth around her nipple and tugged.

"The Were has good instincts."

"Jasyn..."

"Enjoy my love."

He buried his face between her legs, swirling his tongue through her sticky sweet arousal. Heaven. The taste of heaven filled his mouth, and he drank it down greedily. He couldn't get enough.

Her cries were growing more frantic, and Jasyn knew Wyley had moved to her other breast, his hand caressing the soft skin of her stomach. *"Undo his pants, Sheba. Touch him the way you want to touch me."*

She obeyed blindly, too aroused to argue. To think. When he heard the rasp of Wyley's zipper Jasyn slipped two fingers through the soaking folds of Hannah's pussy, dragging them down between her cheeks to press against her ass.

"Fuck. Yeah. *Fuck.*" Wyley's husky groan brought Jasyn's head up. Hannah had taken his cock out of his pants and wrapped her lips around it, sucking him deep into her mouth. Jasyn had never seen anything sexier than Hannah lost to passion.

"Don't stop, Jasyn. Don't stop. I'm so close."

He stood, flipping Hannah onto her stomach. "I can't wait, Sheba. Suck his cock while I watch. While I fuck you."

Wyley slipped out of his jeans and climbed higher on the bed, kneeling in front of Hannah with his cock in hand.

Hannah was dreaming. She had to be. Only she'd never had a sex dream so carnal, so forbidden. Jasyn, her mate, her love, his thick shaft pushing inside her tingling sex—and Wyley, a stranger with a beautiful smile, and an even more beautiful cock that was rock hard and rubbing against her lips. She'd never felt so bad.

"And you love it, don't you, Sheba?"

She did. Goddess help her, but she did. She tried to wrap her small fist around Wyley's erection and guided it to her mouth. Jasyn's hips slung forward, her moan vibrating against Wyley's flesh.

"You're so tight, Sheba. So wet for us." He spread the cheeks of her ass as he thrust against her, his fingers once more teasing her anus. Oh, yes. Yes. She knew what was coming. She wasn't sure she could take it, but she wanted it.

"*You can take it, Sheba. Every last, fucking inch. And you'll love it, mate. Poor Wyley will never feel your touch again, but he'll never forget. Never forget your hot mouth, your tight pussy branding him while I fill your ass with my cock and sink my fangs in deep.*"

The picture he'd painted, along with his hips pumping against hers, was too much for her to take. She came screaming against Wyley's cock, his growl matching Jasyn's as her body rocked between them.

She heard Jasyn's harsh command to the other Were and then she was floating, her nerves still firing, blood boiling with her climax. Jasyn positioned her over Wyley, now laying flat on his back in the middle of the bed.

Hannah gripped the bed frame, loving the firm grip of Jasyn's hands on her hips, the restraint obvious in Wyley's tight jaw as he lay with his hands behind his head. She felt powerful. Desirable. Irresistible.

"All that and more, my Sheba. Take him inside you, baby. Take what you need."

"I need you, Jasyn."

"You have me. I'm right here."

She felt her fangs slice through her gums, her grip on the headboard tightening with every downward thrust of her hips. Having Wyley inside her was different. Good, but different. Not Jasyn.

"You're mine, Sheba. No one else's. Lean forward, and let me show you."

She did as he asked, relaxing at Wyley's gentle smile. "You feel so good, Hannah. It'll be hard to hold myself back."

"But you will." Jasyn's voice was firm behind her.

"But I will." Wyley winked at her, and she laughed breathlessly. The happy sound became a gasp of nervous excitement when the head of Jasyn's cock lined up with her ass.

The room was still, everything focused on this. On him slowly stretching her wide, inch by unbelievable inch, just like he promised. Her body was shaking like a leaf in a hurricane from the foreign sensations. Pain. Pleasure. Ecstasy. Too much.

"Breathe, Sheba. Breathe slow and deep. So deep, honey. I'm in you so deep. I have to move now, honey. I have to..."

He pulled back slowly, lowering her onto Wyley's lap. She could feel his surprised zing of arousal when the drag of his thick cock rubbed against the other Were's inside her. Three voices moaned as one when Jasyn thrust inside her again. Hannah closed her eyes and lost herself, her universe focused only on this, her heart beating to the rhythm her mate set. Warm, male skin was pressed against her lips and she opened her mouth against it, tasting the salty flesh with a small growl. Jasyn.

"Sink those sexy teeth in, Sheba. Bite your mate."

She wanted nothing more. The first swallow of his blood was bliss. Hers. He was hers. His breath on her shoulder made her smile against his arm. She loved his bite, craved it. *"Claim me, Jasyn. Take me. Now."*

His fangs locked onto her shoulder, hips pounding her against the moaning Wyley. Jasyn's control was all but gone. He used the arm she wasn't clinging to and lifted her bodily off of Wyley. She tried to focus, to watch as the handsome Were took his shaft, slick with her juices, into his own hands, his gaze riveted to the mating couple.

Jasyn was up on his knees rocking her against him, the angle pushing him deeper, impossibly deep. "Close. I need you to come for me. Mate. Come for me."

"Love you, Jasyn."

"Sheba. Great Mother. Yes."

Hannah lifted her mouth from his arm and threw back her head, the climax too strong to hold back. Jasyn's shout matched her own, and then he was kissing her, their necks straining as they shared the taste of the other on their tongues.

They clung to each other, bodies rocking gently as they came back down to earth. Without a word Jasyn slid off the bed and carried her to the shower, his lips gliding over the skin within his reach, hands caressing and cleaning every inch of her beneath the hot spray.

"You were beautiful. A goddess."

"You weren't so bad yourself. But I still mean what I said."

He lifted her chin and smiled into her eyes. *"What was that again?"*

"That if you ever want to do that with another woman I'll have to kill you."

He chuckled. *"I'd be insulted if you didn't. And don't get used to this either. This was a one time deal. Although I may owe my brother an apology. And my admiration. Our Alpha obviously has a lot of stamina."*

Hannah lowered her soapy hand between Jasyn's thighs, cupping him with a sassy wink. *"I like your stamina."*

"I love you."

"I know."

Hannah couldn't believe that so much had changed in so short a time. She wrapped the towel around her body and wiped off the moisture to look at herself in the mirror. She felt different. Stronger in so many ways. She'd helped to rescue her friends. Her mate. She'd just had wild sex with two werewolves for goodness sake. She wasn't invisible now.

"Oh, Sheba. You were never invisible. And you've always been strong. I always knew you'd be my perfect mate. I was the one who had to become worthy of you. Now let's go have a drink with our friendly American."

Hannah's heart filled with love for him. This was worth the

wait. Worth everything. They turned toward the bathroom door and she hesitated. Blushing. "I can't believe I feel shy."

"I like you shy. In fact, maybe we should find you some clothes before you go back out there."

She rolled her eyes and pushed past him, almost missing his sly smile. *"There may be such a thing as knowing someone too well."*

"Not in our world, Sheba."

Wyley was already dressed and sitting by the fire, a beer from the mini fridge in his hand. "This loft is bigger than it seems from the outside. Not at all where I would have expected vampires to live though, not a coffin in sight."

Hannah huffed in mock indignation, then joined the two men in their laughter. "It's a lot to take in. Trust me, I know, although after being raised in Hollywood, I was already used to characters."

"Montana has its share of odd humans. But the fact that all this was here, that we never knew. I feel like a goldfish that just realized there was life outside the bowl. Hanging around you folks is one exciting thing after another." He set the beer down and rubbed his hands on his jean-clad thighs in a nervous move before standing. "I just wanted to...thank you, both of you, for allowing me to share..." He gestured toward the rumpled bed, looking at anything but them.

"You aren't the only one who's shy, Sheba."

"We really do need to give him to Nicolette."

"He isn't a present, Hannah. We can nudge, we can't give."

"We should nudge."

Jasyn ignored her and clapped Wyley on the back. "Thank you for helping me fulfill my mate's sordid fantasies." He smirked at her gasp. "You have a loyal ally and home with the

Dydarren Pack for as long as you like."

"I'm honored." Wyley smiled at Hannah, and she knew he was looking for a sign from her that she agreed with her mate. Her answer was to reach up on her toes and kiss his blazing cheek.

Jasyn growled playfully, pulling her back into his arms. "Enough of that, you two. I need to get my Sheba into some clothes and then we should put together something from the kitchen downstairs. I've worked up an appetite."

"Sounds like a plan to me." The relieved Wyley retrieved his beer while Hannah headed toward the closet, thinking to borrow something of Regina's. She'd just pulled on a pair of the Reader's hip hugging black pants and T-shirt when a feeling like a bat to the back of her head knocked her to her knees.

"Hannah." Jasyn was beside her in seconds, searching, a little desperately, for the blood he was sure he would find. But the blow hadn't been physical. It took her a moment for her ears to stop ringing, and the spots to fade from her vision.

It was so weak she almost missed it, as though they had used all of their strength to send a signal, and that was all they had left. "It's Alexei and the twins."

Wyley bent down beside them. "Are they in danger? Are the others? Do they need us?"

Hannah closed her eyes, trying to piece it together. She felt Jasyn beside her, both of them reaching out for the weakening connection. "Yes and no. I don't think they are in immediate danger where they are. But something..." Another burst of power, an unmistakable image exploding behind her lids. "Great Mother. Jasyn."

Jasyn lifted her to her feet, his expression grim. "I saw it. The Shadow Wolves are coming. And they aren't alone."

Hannah grabbed her knotted stomach, fear chilling her

blood. "From what Alexei is sending, more than we've ever seen in one place."

Wyley stood up and strode swiftly over to the couch, grabbing his hat. "I told you. One exciting thing after another." They watched him settle his cowboy hat in a rakish slant on his head, his grin bloodthirsty. "What are we waiting for? It looks like a storm is brewing with our name on it."

Hannah couldn't share his eagerness. Without her temporary abilities, she wasn't strong, couldn't affect nature. Nothing. She certainly didn't know how to fight. How could she help the children? Nicolette?

Jasyn gripped her shoulders and shook her lightly. "Hannah, you are Were. When the time comes, if it comes, instinct will kick in. Trust me."

Wyley nodded. "He's right, Miss Hannah. Besides, if any of them touch you, your mate and I will rip off their arms and use their claws for back scratchers."

Jasyn's lip curled in response. "I do like the way he thinks. I only wish Kit and Arygon were here as well. If the little guy is right, this will be one hell of a battle."

A battle. She hadn't even shifted yet, was barely mated. She could only hope her instincts didn't taken a vacation right when she needed them the most.

Chapter Nine

Midnight was nervous, but if Liz wasn't in his mind, she wouldn't have known it from his expressionless face. She could only imagine how hard this must be for him, returning home.

"This was never my home, Lizbeth. Not since I was a child."

Since his mother left. Another story Malcolm had never shared. She was away. Traveling. That was the only excuse she heard when she was first introduced to his family. Midnight's memories were different. His father had sent their mother away, determined that she would not weaken his heirs with her mothering. To keep his own secrets safe, Elder Abaddon had held her children hostage. Liz already hated the twisted old jackass. Now more than ever.

The six of them—Zander and Regina, Lux and Sylvain, she and Midnight walked through the gate without incident, leaving the few Sariel guards they had with them to disappear into the shadows around the house. She knew the others were only thinking of their children, worrying for their safety. Liz was as well, but she was more concerned about her *grathita*. Memories continued to flood into his mind. And the closer he got, the darker they became.

The blood servant opened the door, a new one, Liz noted, but just as emaciated and haggard as the last. "You are expected. Please go through to the Great Room, Elder Abaddon will be with you shortly." He turned and disappeared swiftly around the corner, leaving them unattended in the foyer.

She was seeing the house through new eyes. Midnight's eyes. Things were different. The statues that had been added, each one more horrific and ridiculous than the next. The painting on the ceiling had been halfway finished the last time he'd seen it. But he could still see himself running up the main stairs as a child, laughing with his brother as they played hide and seek with their cousins.

"Goddess, I hate this place." Regina flinched, looking over at Midnight apologetically. "I just...well the last time I was here..."

"Don't upset yourself, Reader. I hold no fondness for this place or its occupants." They walked toward the Great Room, reaching out with their senses for any sign of Nicolette or the children. "And the feeling is mutual, as you can see from this warm family reunion."

He opened the door and headed inside, stopping dead at the sight of the imposing wall-sized oil painting that was the focal point of the room. It was an image of the Great War, the war between the Shadow Wolves and the Truebloods. Malcolm Abaddon stood victorious on the battlefield, bodies strewn at his feet, his hand raised to the swirling storm above him.

"Storm Bringer." Midnight's whisper was full of emotion. Longing. Sadness. Regret. Liz slid her arm through his and leaned her head on his shoulder. Lux and Zander came to stand beside them.

Zander spoke in a low, solemn voice. "They say the Truebloods would have fallen into chaos without him. Before he took command, taking the fight to the *Les Loup De La Hombre*, the Trust was not unified as to what course of action to take, and the clans themselves were hesitant to act. He brought everyone together, fought with a ferocity none had seen before or since, and laid the Shadow low."

Lux nodded. "He was a hero. A leader."

"He was a lunatic bent on revenge. And now you've come back to kill me, haven't you, Marcos? Come back to kill me for what I did to him. Knew you'd come. Knew it all along."

Midnight closed his eyes for a moment, turning with a sardonic smile to greet the small, agitated man on the other side of the room. "I missed you, too, Father. I'm glad we had this opportunity to catch up on old times. Now where is Nicolette?"

Elder Abaddon tilted his head, gripping the chair at the head of the long table, talking to the painting instead of Midnight. "Was it my fault you wouldn't do what you were told? Wouldn't back down? Now Sebastian and Sari are dead. And my Nicolette, what will they do to my Nicolette? All because of you."

Zander rounded the meeting table and gripped the elder's robes, nearly lifting him off the floor. "Old man, you have never been the sanest of vampires, but you were a respected Trueblood once. A man with a modicum of honor. We know Nicolette came here. Tell us where she is. Now."

Abaddon's face screwed up, his eyes bulging as he struggled in Zander's grip. "Sullied your blood line with a Reader. Thought they were all gone. Just a myth. If you hadn't been so like your father we could have used you. But you were good. Too good. Killed Grey Wolf. And my Sebastian's dead." Abaddon started to weep and Zander sighed, lowering his flailing feet back to the floor.

"He isn't making sense. Nothing he's thinking is making any sense. It's like there are more—" Regina's golden gaze met Liz's, sharing the unbelievable possibility forming in her mind. "Zander, remove his robes."

"Nooooo!" Abaddon tried to run but he tripped over his own bedraggled hem, falling to the ground. Zander didn't hesitate. He slipped a hand beneath the neckline of the once elaborate robe and shredded it down the middle, baring the writhing man's back for all to see.

"Great Mother, protect us."

"Aren't those—shit."

Liz followed Midnight as Lux and Sylvain exclaimed in horror. Liz was feeling a little queasy herself. She'd never seen anything like it. The elder was covered with the marks of the Shadow. Tattooed from head to toe. The only skin that could be seen was riddled with bite marks and deep scarring. Layers on layers of scarring. The body was unable to heal when the old magic was infused into the skin. The scar that had curved across Midnight's face was fading with the marks on his neck, but it was nothing compared to what had been done to his father.

Abaddon rolled over, revealing a front just as mutilated as his back. Liz joined Midnight as he knelt down beside his father. He was confused. What did this mean? The man he'd seen as the epitome of evil, possibly even a leader of *asura saMsaki*, was instead a victim? Or had he given his body willingly to the Shadow Wolves?

Wild, milky eyes lifted to Midnight's. "Damn the Goddess and her curse. Why did She make me love her? And now it's too late. All our children are dead. We will all be dead when the others arrive. We're all dead!" Insane laughter choked him, blood and spittle flying out of his cracked, thin lips.

Midnight lifted him off the floor, into his arms while his father continued to gasp for air. He didn't flinch when the scars on the old man's body opened anew, as though they were fresh wounds, gushing with what little blood he had left.

"He's dying. Oh, Zander. The thoughts in his mind." Liz heard Regina sobbing behind her, knew they were all there, watching helplessly as this man, regardless of how he'd lived his life, was slowly dying an agonizing death.

Midnight set him down gently, carefully on his side so he wouldn't choke on his own blood, before standing to join the others. Liz felt her own heart breaking for all her mate had lost. And for what? It seemed they were further away from the answers than ever.

"I'm so sorry, my love."

"You're my family, wildcat. This man is a stranger to me."

He turned to the others, his hands covered in blood, his eyes dark with suppressed rage. "He's not dead yet, but he's in no position to stop us. This house is a labyrinth. If we're going to find the children and Nicolette, we need to start now."

"I don't understand why they're still blocking us. Hiding from us."

Regina took Sylvain's hand. "I don't think it's us they are hiding from. We aren't alone here. Even now it feels like someone, or some thing is watching us. The elder's last thoughts before he fell unconscious were of Nicolette. And another woman with dark hair and,"—she glanced up at Midnight, an apology in her eyes, —"eyes just like yours."

"My mother. It's nice to know he is thinking of her at the end."

"You don't understand, Midnight. It was recent. He was seeing them together. And Nicolette wasn't in very good shape." Zander pulled Regina closer when Midnight snarled, rejecting her words.

Liz put a hand on his arm. "He is crazy. Not making any sense. We don't know if his mind was playing tricks on him. Whatever the case, we have to find Nic and the children, and get the hell out of this asylum."

Midnight nodded, heading toward the painting on the wall. "Whose idea was it to put this picture here?"

Liz's brow furrowed at the unusual question. "Malcolm's. They wanted to hang it in Haven, or the main entry to the manor, but Mal talked them out of it. He said he wanted to be on display in his favorite room in the house."

Midnight's chuckle was grim as he pulled the frame off the wall, smearing it with blood and tilting it on its side in the corner. "Malcolm hated this room. We studied here, stuck inside when all he wanted to do was roam the grounds and play pirate. That is of course, until we found it."

Lux caught the painting before it fell to the marble floor. "Found what?"

Midnight smacked the lower portion of the wall with the flat of his hand, smiling when a panel slid open, revealing a small, narrow tunnel. "Our special place. I'm sure Father and other members of the family knew about it. But at the time we thought we'd discovered the greatest secret of all time. It's a tunnel that leads to nearly every room in the house." He caught Zander's gaze with his own. "Including mine."

"Alexei." Regina tried to push him aside to enter the tunnel and find her child, but Midnight stopped her. "Let me go, *please*. I need to find him. Need to make sure he's okay."

"I go first." Liz watched his gaze land once more on Abaddon's body, and she saw a memory that wasn't her own. A day he'd hid behind this panel, listening to his father talk to a female blood servant as though she were his mother, calling her by his mother's name as he beat her and forced her to submit to his will. Midnight hated him then. Hated him because he knew that his mother was witnessing the abuse through their blood connection. That in this way, Abaddon was punishing her as well as the weeping human.

He'd promised himself at that moment that he would pay his father back. That he wouldn't rest until he saw him suffering as much as he'd made her suffer. But he felt no satisfaction today.

He turned and ducked into the opening, with Liz and the others following quickly behind. Claustrophobia set in almost immediately. She felt vulnerable, trapped, crawling on her hands and knees through a tunnel barely large enough for Alexei.

"It seemed bigger when I was young."

"I don't know why we couldn't have gone up the stairs."

"Did you miss the Reader's words? We are not alone. Better to take them by surprise than fall into a trap."

"Unless this is the trap."

"I thought I was the cynical half of this mating."

She stuck her tongue out toward his perfect, irritating ass, unable to stop the thrill of joy she got from making him laugh, even in a situation like this. She would have continued the banter, but something made her and the others freeze in the cramped tunnel. Barely discernible, even to her ears. A cry for help.

"It's Nicolette." Sylvain's whisper reached Liz just as the call came again, louder this time, from a panel just ahead.

Midnight spoke over his shoulder. "You go on, straight and up until the tunnel splits and go left. If they're where I think they are, the children should be in the small alcove behind the panel to Malcolm's and my suite. I'll get Nicolette."

"I'm going with you." Liz had opened her mouth to say the words, but surprisingly, they'd come from Zander. "You shouldn't have to go in alone." He smiled at Liz. "Either of you."

Regina nodded at Liz, showing her agreement. She knew that her little Gypsy had a hand in the Mediator's decision. If what she'd seen was correct, Midnight might have to face more than he bargained for to save Nicolette.

"Sure, leave me with the women. It doesn't affect my masculinity in the slightest." Lux chuckled, but Liz knew he was worried about sending his brother down there alone.

"I leave my child and *grathita* in your care, brother. I wouldn't be able to do this otherwise."

Liz knew Midnight was listening to the Sariel brothers' exchange intently. It made him think of Malcolm for a moment, before he pushed it aside to focus on the coming task.

Midnight slid open the panel, and Liz looked over his shoulder. Another tunnel, this one descending sharply. It was one he didn't remember. *"But how is that possible? I lived in these tunnels as a child. I knew where all of them led."*

She didn't know. But a strange foreboding shuddered down her spine as the unmistakable scent wafted up the shaft. Shadow.

"I smell it too. You should go with—"

"The women? Don't say it, Midnight. Don't even think it."

"I forgot I bound myself to a modern female warrior."

"Don't forget again."

"Yes, my love."

They had to turn themselves around, crawling in feet first and using the sides to stop them from crashing to the bottom. Her arms trembled, not just from the effort, but adrenaline. Midnight's adrenaline. His emotions were in turmoil, the loudest and most powerful among them was anger. Anger at what had been done to him, to his family. The reasons didn't matter at this moment. Only the scent of his enemy.

"They're here. Oh thank the Goddess, the three of them are scared. But safe. There are a few men with guns on the other side of the panel. I can read them. They won't be there for long."

Liz heard Zander's breath huff out in a small moan of relief that quickly changed to worry. They didn't move for long moments, waiting to hear from Regina again.

"We're locked in Midnight's room. Alexei isn't very responsive, like he's in some kind of trance, but Pax told me he is concentrating. That the danger isn't over yet. Lux is looking him over, making sure he's okay. Get Nicolette so we can take him home."

Liz closed her eyes. At least the children were safe. She had a feeling this wouldn't be the last time Alexei drove his parents sick with worry. That child was too powerful for his own good.

"Don't worry, Lizbeth. I have a feeling he'll be the best Mediator in our history. No one will dare naysay him."

"Maybe. Or he could become a master criminal. Only time will tell."

Midnight stopped before the end of the tunnel, studying the square of wood that was their exit. His body tensed, using his arms to gather momentum. Liz closed her eyes when the power of his boots splintered the panel into pieces.

She followed him through, wishing she had Mal's dagger. Even with her new Trueblood abilities, the damp limestone cavern filled ankle-deep with stagnant water made her nervous.

"Help us! Please help us!" The plea was much louder now. Louder, and no longer Nicolette's. She sounded terrified, and Liz took an instinctive step forward.

"Wait, Lizbeth. Go slow. All is not as it seems."

Zander was the last to come out of the shaft, moving to stand beside Liz, looking around the cavernous sinkhole with disgust. The smell *was* nauseating. Shadow and rotting death all around. "This place is disgusting. Regina says she thinks the rest of the top floor is empty, but I won't feel safe until my family is off Abaddon land completely."

Midnight spoke over his shoulder, his gaze intent on the darkness. "Tell her not to let her guard down. I know his security and blood servants haven't all been accounted for yet. And be quiet. Our conversation is no longer private."

"Is someone there? I know you aren't Shadow Wolf. There's another woman with me, and she's hurt. I killed one of his blood servants, but that...that monster will be back any minute."

The woman sounded frantic. Hopeful. They moved closer, stepping slowly over the dead body of the servant who had let them in. Liz flinched. A single ray of bluish moonlight came from a hole in the ground high above them and landed on two women huddled together on a large, smooth rock that sat like an island in a sea of filth.

She was crying, her head buried in Nicolette's long blonde hair as she rocked the Unborn in her arms. Liz took a hasty, splashing step forward. *Nicolette*. The woman looked up at the sound. "At last. I've been here so long. Kept away from my husband and children. You don't know what that *thing* has made me do."

Zander quickened his pace. "Let us help you. My name is Zander Sariel. We need to get the two of you to safety."

"Zander...Alexander's son?" The woman sobbed in relief, turning her face up to him with a radiant smile and indigo eyes that made Liz stumble. There were lines on her face that came from age and grief, but she was stunning. And she looked like Midnight. "I remember when you were just a baby. My twins, Sebastian and Sari were born not long after your mother had you. My name is Miriam. Miriam Abaddon."

"No. Don't listen to her. Sh-she lies." Nicolette's head rolled back, revealing the once flawless face covered with bruises and claw marks.

The woman holding her lost her helpless, hapless expression in an instant, rolling her familiar eyes. "All you had to do was stay quiet for a few more minutes. Was that too much to ask? I was trying to save you. After all, in a round about way, you did bring my son back home to me."

Nicolette looked directly at Liz and tried to smile as, before anyone had a chance to move, Miriam punched a clawed hole through her heart.

"Nicolette!" Midnight lifted Liz's struggling body off her feet, not allowing her to rush to her friend's body as it slid off the rock and into the water, facedown. It made no sense. She couldn't accept it. She wasn't gone. How could Nicolette be gone? She was family. How would the Deva Clan—how would *she* survive without her? Cold shock filled her stomach, her limbs. And the other woman was...smiling? "Why? Why would you do that? Nicolette! Let me go, damn you. I need to help her. Great Mother, *why*?"

"I think I just told her, were you not paying attention?" Miriam's expression was smug as she looked at Midnight. "She's always been a little slow, Marcus. If she wasn't perhaps my heroic Malcolm would still be alive. But then I never could understand my sons' taste in women."

Midnight set Liz down between himself and Zander, making sure the Mediator kept hold of his struggling, shouting mate. *"It's not safe, Lizbeth. I need you with me. Focus on what's in front of us."*

His enigmatic gaze never strayed from the woman who had been his mother. "You dare lay claim to us? You earn my gratitude for my delivery into this world, but only contempt for your absence."

Liz knew he was trying to be strong, for her. She forced her eyes forward, knowing she couldn't look at Nicolette's lifeless body and remain standing. Midnight knew it too. So he put aside his own feelings of shock and betrayal as he stood in front of his murderous mother. For her.

Miriam was standing, her gown glittering in the soft light. "I've never been far from my children. But I am not just a mother. I am a woman. My heart was torn in two between my love for you, and my love for my mate."

"Your mate lays bleeding to death in the house above. For all his cruelty he did not abandon his duties." Zander spoke through gritted teeth, his hands gripping Liz's shoulders tightly. They were all walking a tight thread. All working so hard not to let the rage and grief distract them from this dangerous viper in their midst.

She laughed at Zander. "You *are* Alexander's son. So proper. So smug and superior. But you have no right to judge me. *Your* mate is an abomination. But the Clan Trust accepted her. Why? Because you are a Sariel." She spit out the name like a curse. "Pure blood. Pure rubbish. And your brother. Don't make me laugh. His mates, both Weres, welcomed into the Trueblood community like brethren."

Her voice rose, the sound harsh and ugly. "*I* was denied my place. Denied my children. But that perverse puff of a vampire you call brother is hailed as the fulfiller of the Mother's Message. As if *he* were the only Trueblood in history to have two mates."

Midnight stepped closer before Zander could lose his temper. "You have a lot of information for someone in hiding. What did you mean when you said Nicolette brought me home to you?"

Her expression softened to one of motherly devotion. Though the glint in her eyes was far from maternal. "Do you know until this last year I was sure you were dead? All my children gone. When we started getting reports of you again, I was overjoyed. You came out first, you know. Before Malcolm. My firstborn son. And my champion. I know how you defended me to your father. It warmed my heart."

"Is that why you didn't simply have me killed when I got close to discovering the members of *asura saMsaki*? A mother's love?"

"No. It is why *I* didn't kill you. I strive eternally for my mate's happiness." The large grizzled man came out of the darkness, dragging a bloodied sword behind him. "I got rid of the Sariel guard who followed her, dearest. He won't need this anymore." The two laughed together, and Liz fell to her knees in the rancid water. Max. That was his sword. Great Mother, had he killed Max?

Midnight couldn't move. The final piece of the puzzle had snapped into place at the Shadow's arrival. He remembered his last night as Marcus Abaddon.

"Do you swear to honor the secrecy of the Demon Coalition, to carry to your eternal grave all that you witness here tonight?"

"I do."

"We've watched you closely. The reason we didn't contact you sooner was the bond of brotherhood you share with your brother, Malcolm. He is not like us. He actually likes humans, believes we can live together peacefully." The elder sneered, watching Marcus closely to gauge his reaction.

"My brother and I shared a womb. That is all. The path he follows is not mine. I want none of it." May the Goddess forgive his lie. He calmed his heart rate, refusing to look away until the older man blinked.

He was so close.

That his father was involved was not something he doubted. But how far did this cult of theirs go? Was it more than just a club of discontented Truebloods? Were they actually in league with the Shadow Wolves? Were the rumors of murder and political intrigue true? His answers lay beyond a thick metal door. And this masked man had the key.

"It is time." Marcus grasped his hands behind his back, striving for the appearance of ennui. He was a young, rich, jealous Trueblood. Twin brother to one of the most influential man in a generation. A man everyone looked up to. A man above suspicion. The perfect cover.

He entered a room bare of any wall hangings or decoration. A group of hooded men in masks surrounded the only furniture in the room. An altar. "Let me guess. We're slaughtering goats before we head out to the secret masquerade ball."

No one appeared surprised by his irreverence. He hadn't expected them to. He'd played the bad boy for too long for an immediate change to be believable. The man beside him laughed. "Not exactly, Marcus. This is part of the welcoming ritual. You will lie upon the altar and answer the members' questions. When they have been answered to our satisfaction, we will relax, play with our beautiful blood servants, and talk of war."

There was no way he could get out of this gracefully. A few questions, and he would be accepted as one of them. A small price to pay. He walked at a leisurely pace, studying each cloaked man in turn.

His father couldn't be among them. This time. Surely by now he would have reacted to his son's disrespectful behavior.

He knew there were a handful of Elders in the crowd, but who were the others? His peers? His relatives?

He lay down on the altar, his hands folded across his chest and a smirk on his face. "Shall we begin?"

They dove on him with a speed he hadn't foreseen, pulling his hands down at his side and closing the shackles over his wrists and ankles. "Bloody bastards, what in the name of—" A cloth saturated with a strong herbal narcotic filled his mouth, too deep for him to spit out.

And then he saw them. The crowd parted and he saw his father, a maniacal gleam in his eyes. Beside him stood a large Werewolf, snarling at the cowering crowd. He shifted into a muscular man, and Marcus saw his father hand the Shadow Wolf a cloak.

"Thank you Elder Abaddon. For this, and so many other things. You should go now." And without a word his father turned, as though on strings, and disappeared around the corner.

"Did you think you were so clever, young Abaddon? Did you think we would not see through you? That we would be so careless when there is so much at stake?" The Shadow *tsked*, shaking his head in gentle reprisal. "You are a boy playing spy, but this is a man's game. And your father, our leader, has given the order."

The man nodded and the others stepped back, giving him room to move around Marcus's body. He leaned in close. "Your mother sends her love." Marcus jerked against his restraints, fighting the drug and the Shadow smiled. "You should see the look on your face. Better yet, you should see the look on hers each night as I take her. Unfortunately even if you had, you wouldn't remember it after tonight. You'll forget all of this. Your family. Your dear, sainted brother. And he will weep. For you.

He will be so inconsolable that he won't notice until the wolf is at the door. And then, it will be too late."

The Shadow straightened and lashed out with his claws, a deep scarlet slash down Marcus's cheek. "A little something to remember us by." He was still laughing when Marcus slipped into unconsciousness.

He came back to the present on a wave of love and pride from his *grathita*, his wildcat. Midnight smiled at his mother's mate, at the man responsible for it all. The monster who had made him. "You had it all figured out, but Malcolm didn't follow your plan, did he? The plan you had worked so hard to bring to fruition? You'd made my father the leader, the scapegoat in case you were caught, you made me the sword that my brother was supposed to throw himself on, and you made fools out of the Truebloods, all for nothing. Malcolm was a warrior. He lived and died as a warrior, and he mourned as a warrior mourns. As the Storm Bringer mourns. And he killed thousands of your people because of what you set in motion. I bet that pissed you off."

The Shadow growled, but Midnight was just getting started. "So you lay low for a while, still guiding things, still ensuring that the old prejudices between Were and Trueblood, natural born and Unborn remain intact. Maybe even help put the idea in Sebastian's head, through your own personal Elder puppet of course, to kill his older brother Malcolm. That would solve all your problems. But then Sebastian's alliance with Grey Wolf gets out of your control, and the Mediator of the Clan Trust mates with, of all creatures, an Unborn Reader. And the Trust actually accepts her. You must have been foaming at your furry little mouth."

"You need to tie up your loose ends now." Midnight stilled

in surprise as Zander took up the narrative. "Maybe his allies are no longer in the Trust, maybe some have had a change of heart. When a Were and Unborn, both connected to the Sariels, start to pick up your trail, you come up with a plan."

"This is where the evil villain lays out his dastardly plan before he kills the hero, giving the hero enough time to devise a way to kill the villain and save the day." Miriam leaned her cheek against her hand dramatically, before shaking her head. "Don't make me laugh. My mate is a genius. He's the true hero. Unlike my *grathita*. Unity my frilly umbrella. The Mother made a mistake. Abaddon is weak. His children were weak. Yvan has a vision for our future. A future that isn't about judgment and rules. And with the paper trail your Nicolette discovered dealt with, the only people who know about us, are you. But that won't matter after tonight."

Midnight shook his head. "I'm not tied up and drugged this time. And I'm not alone. You can't think the two of you can take all of us on."

Yvan wrapped his arm around Miriam and winked. "I could. But I don't have to. As soon as I knew the charms had been broken, we invited a few friends over. You'd be surprised at how many jumped at the chance to slay the Sariels, their mutant mates and the Storm Bringer's twin all in one night. Honestly, you should be flattered."

Midnight was rocked back on his heels when a strong wind blew into the stagnant cave, picking up his mother and her lover and carrying them into the darkness. He chased after them, but the force of the wind blew him back. "Fuck."

"Well, now we know what her element is." Zander came to a stop beside him, kicking the water in helpless rage. "How could we not know? My father? Anyone? All this happening right under our noses, and no one knew."

Midnight turned to make sure his mate was all right. She was kneeling beside Nicolette's body, cradling her in her arms and rocking back and forth. "I don't know, Mediator. But too many people have paid for this secret with their lives. And too many have gotten away with murder. No more."

His *grathita* glanced up at him, tears streaming unheeded down her cheeks. "We have to get her out of here. She deserves better. She didn't deserve this." She took a shaky breath. "And Max. We have to find Max."

"We will, Lizbeth. We will. And then,"—he accepted Zander's hand and got to his feet,—"then we need to prepare for what's coming. Whatever that may be." But he knew the enemy. Knew neither of them would be able to resist witnessing their masterpiece. And he knew what he would have to do before this night was over.

Goddess give him strength.

Chapter Ten

They came together near the standing stones on Abaddon land. Out in the open, to avoid any more surprises. As if they needed more.

Sylvain and the two Sariel guards had rushed the children to the Healer's house. Priestess Magriel and Mysha would protect them with their lives, Hannah knew. None of them took a breath, with Midnight's mother Miriam Abaddon and her Shadow mate Yvan nearby, until Lux turned to them with a relieved smile. "They've arrived safely."

Hannah was still in shock. After the message from Alexei, she, Jasyn and Wyley had come running. They'd almost arrived when she'd stumbled, crying out in pain-filled denial. Nicolette was dead. Her sire. Her mother and friend.

She could see the same heartache and disbelief in Liz and Regina. Nicolette was the glue that had held them all together. That had made their clan of outcasts a family. Having her away in England had been hard enough on the rest of the Unborns. Now Deva castle was in disarray, and she knew it would never be the same. First one of their leaders had become a Trueblood mate, and now this. It wasn't right. The elegant courtesan, who'd faced cruelty as a human, adversity and rejection as a vampire, had never had a chance to find her happiness. Never had the chance to find someone to love her as much as she deserved to be loved.

And now she lay on a bed in Abaddon manor, lifeless. For what?

Lux squeezed Jasyn's shoulder, lifting Hannah's chin with the gentlest of fingers. "We will all grieve for her, Hannah. Madame Nicolette D'Nocturne. For hundreds of years we allowed ourselves to be manipulated." His glance at Midnight was telling. "Allowed innocents to be lost along the way and heroes fall, never knowing there was someone else, something else, pulling the strings."

Liz choked back a sob, and Midnight pulled her into his arms as Lux continued. "Within her first year as the Deva representative for the Clan Trust, she'd not only continued to change the way Truebloods looked at Unborns, she'd uncovered the greatest secret in our history. In doing so, she also gave Midnight back his life, brought Jasyn and Hannah together and saved Elizabeth and the others from falling for yet another deception." He looked at Zander, and lightning streaked across the sky. "She will be honored as a hero."

The Mediator nodded in agreement, and Jasyn pulled Hannah closer. "She saved you for me that day. You would have died in that damn car, and I would never have gotten to you on time. The Weres will honor her as well."

Liz pulled away from Midnight and brushed the tears from her face briskly. "Okay, what about Max?"

"We found blood, but no body. Max is a Sariel guard, an Igigi warrior. I refuse to believe that the older Shadow killed him." Zander's gaze strayed to Midnight. "I am sorry for all you've lost, my friend. But that meeting gave me more questions than answers. I imagine those same markings that kept you from remembering who you were, helped Yvan keep his mate and himself hidden from everyone for all of these years.

Allowing him to remain close without being detected. Maybe it even blocked the normal bond between mother and child. My question is, why did they want you coming back?"

Wyley, who'd maintained a respectful distance as they grieved for their friend, stepped forward, his hands deep in the pockets of his jeans. "No Shadow came to my mountain for centuries that I knew of. Not during your war or after. Not until this past year. Why? And what about Jasyn and Nicolette? They could've killed them easily enough, but they brought Jasyn across the ocean and chained him up in Midnight's territory, where he'd be sure to find them, leaving a trail you'd have to follow."

"I believe we are thinking along the same lines, Were."

Jasyn swore under his breath. "I was bait."

Lux flinched. "It sounds like it, doesn't it. With Nicolette so close to Regina and Liz, and you my *grathita's* brother, they knew we would come for Midnight and someone would recognize him, either as Malcolm's double, or Marcus Abaddon himself. They wanted us to bring him home."

Hannah jumped when Midnight growled and lashed out, punching a chunk out of the smooth stone beside him. "None he sent could do the job, I was too alert, an animal. An animal not distracted as easily as a man returning to remember all he'd lost."

Liz held Midnight's face in her hands, forcing him to look at her. "Then he's made the same mistake twice over. We'll just have to remind him how a warrior mourns."

Hannah leaned back against Jasyn, moved by the love Liz felt for Midnight shining through her eyes. Was it only a few months ago that she believed Liz hard? Someone who kept herself away from emotions? Now she stood here, pushing aside her grief over the loss of her friend for Midnight. Her adoration and pride in her *grathita* clear for all to see.

"*Love has a way of doing that to people, Sheba.*"

"*I'm afraid, Jasyn. I don't think I can lose anymore people I love today.*"

"*I won't let that happen. I promise.*"

"Am I late?"

"It's about damned time, Arygon." Hannah felt Jasyn's surprise at the sight of his brother climbing onto the small rise. The gorgeous Were didn't stop until he'd reached Lux. He took the Trueblood Healer into his arms and kissed him with an unrestrained passion that made her blush.

She couldn't help but sneak a glance at Wyley, wondering how the Were would deal with seeing the two men so open in their need for each other. The interest in his eyes was unexpected.

"*Don't even think it, mate. Our experimenting days with others are over.*"

"It never crossed my mind."

Lux pulled back, his face flushed with desire. "I'm glad you're here. Sylvain has missed you."

"Only Sylvain?" Arygon's wicked smile turned somber as he looked toward Hannah and Jasyn. "My new sister, I'm sorry for your loss. Nicolette was one of a kind. And I can promise you that her killer will pay."

"That is my promise to make." Midnight's words were low, but everyone heard them. Arygon nodded respectfully toward the Trueblood, as though instantly recognizing a fellow leader.

Arygon greeted Zander. "The strongest Weres of our pack are moments behind me. We left this morning to bring my mate and children home. Halfway here, Alexei and the twins sent me a signal that nearly knocked me over with its power. They showed me what was coming. Whatever the Shadow brings, we are ready."

Hannah gasped. "The same thing happened to me. That's how I knew we needed to leave Haven."

Zander sighed, his worried gaze finding Regina's. "Your son."

She shook her head and smiled at her mate. "Our son."

Jasyn slid his hands down to cup Hannah's stomach. *"I can't wait to see you pregnant with our child."*

"Neither can I. Although I've just decided that he or she is not allowed to play with Alexei."

"Agreed."

A roaring, churning mass of sound erupted just beyond the trees in the distance. Hannah knew what it was with a single inhalation. Shadow. And vampire. She felt herself panicking. How would she shift? As an Unborn she just had to think of her totem animal, embrace it in her mind and she changed swiftly, painlessly. Weres were different. It looked painful.

"I won't lie and say it doesn't hurt the first time. But once you get the hang of it, it's almost pleasurable."

"I bet you say that to all the Shebas you bite and turn into werewolves."

"You're my one and only Sheba. Just open your mind and let the Were come out. She's already there. Waiting. You are already joined."

She sensed Wyley moving closer, the two Weres flanking her on either side as they changed. She closed her eyes, hearing the jarring sound of bones cracking and muscles stretching.

Open my mind. Open my mind. How could she open her mind when the Shadows were on their way, sounding like thunder rolling through the quiet night air? But then she sensed her. The Were. A wolf pacing in a cage. A beautiful beast with the need to avenge Nicolette's death. The need to draw blood.

Pain. Every cell in her body exploding and reforming. She felt each follicle open as hair grew on her hands, her face. Her arms and legs were broken and repaired from one heartbeat to the next. She'd never felt anything like it. Hannah was screaming but the Were was howling in delight. Freedom. Strength.

Power.

She opened her eyes, seeking her mate. She looked down. And down. Jasyn and Wyley, fully transformed into the werewolves that had always intimidated her with their size and ferocity, were half her size. How was that possible?

"Sheba, honey, I forgot to tell you..."

"Tell me what?"

"More often than not, female Weres are, well—"

"Bigger. Go on. You can say it."

"It's kind of emasculating that my mate could pick me up and carry me around like a chew toy."

"You do look edible. Jasyn, I feel different. I feel her."

"Embrace it, love. But stay close. They're nearly here."

She saw Regina and Liz looking up at her in shock and gave a toothy smile, feeling more confident than she had in a long time. It was good to be Were.

"Ah, how I love you, my Sheba."

"Back atcha, Big Daddy."

Midnight wondered if this was how Malcolm had felt before his first battle. A rage so intense it gave him clarity. Serenity.

They had taken his life, killed his brother, destroyed his father. His father. How different would his life had been if Elder Abaddon had been in control of his own actions? He would never know.

It was all about control. The *asura saMsaki* was an illusion. The Clan Trust was an illusion. The Shadow had been playing with them all along. And his mate, Midnight's mother, had helped him. They would have to kill him to escape him now.

"Are you still with me, Midnight?"

"You are the only thing that keeps me here."

"Look around you, my love. You have family. Friends. You're not alone anymore."

"Grathita. *I have a lot to make up for.*"

"Then let's kick some flea-bitten ass so we can get started."

"You are a wildcat."

"But I'm your wildcat. You lucky bloodsucker."

He couldn't help but smile. She'd done that for him. Even with her own heart aching at the loss of her friend, she reminded him what happiness felt like. What he was fighting for. What he hadn't felt since he and his twin had been teenagers.

Midnight stepped in front of the others as a sea of Shadow Wolves emerged from the darkness. Vampires who'd shifted into cats and wolves, even birds of prey flew overhead, all slowing as they caught sight of the small gathering at the standing stones. He sensed Arygon's Weres circling behind them, waiting for the order to attack.

His voice rang out over the rolling green landscape. "Hear me. Tonight you have a choice. You don't have to listen to the Shadow that cowers behind you like a child, forcing you to fight his battles. It is Yvan I want. Him alone. You can turn and leave now, and live to fight another day."

The people beside him understood. He was giving them a chance. But the Shadow below roared their answer, some Truebloods laughing in contempt at the option. "What's our other choice?"

He heard the question, despite the cacophony, and smiled. They'd already made it. "I was hoping you'd ask. The other choice is nothing you haven't experienced before. Defeat. Humiliation. Death. Some of you may know of the Storm Bringer. I am his brother. Midnight Fog."

He lifted his hands, and the fog rolled in like a thick blanket around them. He made sure it didn't envelop those behind him, only his enemies. He heard the whip strike of lightning, saw it pierce the fog and heard an angry howl. Lux Sariel. He nodded to Arygon, who'd transformed into a large, silver Were beside him, and the battle began.

There were hundreds of them. He felt his mate's surprise at the number, but he'd known. If the Shadow did anything well, it was hide. Only attacking when there was no other recourse. Or when they believed the Shadow had the advantage. The numbers were definitely in their favor this time. But Midnight knew they'd underestimated the enemy at their peril.

The Mediator had shifted into a large, golden bear, his strength more than a match for the attacking Shadow. Lightning flashed around them, precision strikes that left the smell of charred hide lingering in the air. And Liz was glorious. He couldn't help but keep an eye on her as her jaguar leapt in the air to grasp and ravage a shifted Trueblood hawk.

"I can handle myself. You're the one who needs to focus."

Yes. He had to find Yvan and Miriam. He knew they were here. And if he had to slaughter every last Shadow to find them, that's what he would do. Old instincts took over and he was the

Cursed One again, an animal without mercy.

A Trueblood who had chosen the wrong side shifted back into human form when Midnight wrapped his hand around his throat. "*Please.* I'm one of you. Please don't hurt me!"

"Another Trueblood might be moved by your heartfelt plea." *Snap.* "Sadly, I am not that kind of bloodsucker."

A female Were whimpered in pain, and Midnight whirled around to see Jasyn's mate surrounded. Her left shoulder was bleeding, but she was doing a good job of fending the Shadow off, flinging one and then another into the air with a swing of her good paw.

Jasyn and Wyley were rabid in their efforts to get to her, but this group obviously had a plan. Separate and surround the female. He knew a Shadow woman was not allowed many rights, their size and abilities might have something to do with that. But it also made her the biggest target on a fog-filled battlefield.

Midnight walked swiftly through the mass of claws and flesh, leaving a wave of dropping bodies in his wake. He knew it worried his *grathita*, how easily killing came to him. But right now, he was exactly what the situation called for.

Hannah had been knocked to the ground. He wouldn't get to her soon enough. Jasyn roared in rage, tearing through the circling pack, fur and flesh shredding in his frenzy to get to his mate.

He was so focused on the drama unfolding in front of him that the attack took him by surprise. He saw Jasyn reach his mate just as a clawed hand came around from behind and scraped across his neck, bending him forward when he gripped it instinctively. Another deep cut sliced into his side, throwing him to the ground.

"*Midnight! No!*"

His mate's call made him curse and struggle against the Shadows piling on top of him. They howled for help. They had him. Had the Storm Bringer's twin. Time to go for the kill.

As his Lizbeth would say, "Fuck that."

He bent his knees, kicking out with all his power and rolling until he was free of their weight. The wounds hurt, but they weren't life threatening. The fool Weres hadn't slashed deep enough.

"You can give them lessons in how to kill you later."

"I do need to find some useful employment now that I'm back."

The Shadow who'd jumped him was racing his way, in a blood frenzy that nothing but death or killing could cure. Midnight prepared to give him the former, his hands outstretched to fling the bastard over his head.

The silver glint shimmered in the periphery of his vision followed by the ringing tone of a sword sent the Shadow's head rolling toward Midnight's feet, the body dropping where it stood.

"You didn't think I'd let you have all the fun, did you?"

"Kit!"

"I could have taken him. I don't owe your giant ex-lover anything."

"You're being a baby."

Midnight snarled. "Thanks." He wrestled with the nearest Shadow Wolf, tearing out his heart with one well-aimed strike. "I'm glad your wife let you come over to play."

Kit raised a good humored eyebrow, his already large body growing head and shoulders over the fighters around him, knocking two oncoming Shadows together like coconuts, and tossing them aside. "Are you kidding? I had to tie Jesse up to get her not to leave Priestess Magriel's. We should hurry before they untie her, so I can take advantage of all her pent up frustration myself. Where's Max?"

Midnight couldn't conceal his flinch at the question, and Kit grew even larger. He shook his head. "Guardian, we don't know where Max is. A body was never found. But a Shadow had his sword."

"No body? Bah. Then he lives. And we will end this. *Now!*" The last word, bellowed from his mouth blew a line of Shadow back several steps. He looked down at Midnight and winked. "I brought playmates."

"Midnight, look. Thank the Goddess. The cavalry has arrived. Kit and Sylvain brought the clans."

He looked behind them to see a large group charging toward them. Lizbeth was right. Young and old, the allied clans had come to witness, to be a part of the battle. Leading them with her long, silver hair flying behind her like a flag was Lux and Arygon's mate Sylvain. The *Antara*, they called her. The tiny, waiflike creature lifted up her hand, and he watched as a boulder pulled itself from the earth to fly into the shrieking crowd of attackers.

"Bloody hell."

"Isn't she cute?" Kit laughed as he skewered two comers at once, pushing him off his sword with a grimace. "My wife is half godling, but at least she can't skewer me with a redwood when she's mad. If it wasn't so blasted foggy you could see what the Reader can do. What she did to Grey Wolf. Although if you listen closely, you can hear their screams of utter terror."

He could. He knew from Lizbeth the Gypsy's awesome power. He was grateful that she had killed the bastard who'd seen to Malcolm's death, but he wasn't sure he wanted to witness it firsthand.

Damned if he wasn't starting to like the tall bastard.

"Aw. You're making friends."

"I should have taken a page from his book and tied you up for the duration."

"You can do it later."

His woman. She was fighting at Regina and Zander's side, every inch a warrior. Malcolm would have been proud. He felt a wave of love and gratitude fill his heart.

"*He would have been proud of both of us... Fuck. I see them. Miriam and Yvan. I see them.*"

Without a word to Kit, Midnight spun around in mid air, following the direction of his mate's gaze. His mother's indigo glare clashed with his.

And the wind started to blow.

The fog dissipated, showing without doubt that the tide had turned to their advantage. Bodies littered the ground. Shadow. Half their number lay dead or dying on the wet grass around them. And watching from the safety of the trees as his own people were being mutilated was the coward himself. Yvan.

He was pacing back and forth, watching as his genius plan fell through. Again. But Miriam wasn't paying any attention to her mate. The focus of her anger was all directed at one person. Her firstborn son. Midnight.

Yvan didn't notice when she walked toward the fighting, too busy shaking his fist at a nearby Trueblood, pointing to Sylvain and the other clan members. They met in the middle and she created a funnel of air around them, sealing them off from the rest of the world. "You're an Abaddon. Why won't you just die?"

She sounded truly dumbfounded. She didn't understand how he'd survived all she'd put him through. To be honest, neither did he, but it wasn't exactly what you wanted to hear the woman who gave birth to you say. "Perhaps I'm too much like my father. Why would you do all of this, go to all this trouble just to ensure the last of your offspring dies?"

"I'm not a monster, Marcus. Do you think I would do all this just to kill you? Of course, killing you is a necessary evil. But Yvan's vision is so much grander than that. The treaty they were about to sign cannot happen. Since the *asura saMsaki* had lost its influence, and your pathetic father has been seen for the insane twit he is, we had to create chaos. Yvan decided we could solve all our problems if we killed the Reader and the Antara, the mates of the Alpha Were and Mediator."

"That plan seems to be working out for you splendidly."

Miriam slapped him across the face. "Show some respect. If you'd truly been worthy, you could have joined us. But I knew how much you loved your brother. Knew you would never betray him."

Midnight felt the last shred of love he had for her turn to dust. "Have you ever felt that way about anyone? How could I have been so wrong about you?"

Tears welled up in her strange swirling eyes. "I loved you with all my heart. I even believed I loved your father. Until I met Yvan. Then I understood what passion was. Excitement. And I knew I would never be happy unless I was with him."

Much as he didn't want to, he understood. She was twisted. Psychotic. But she did understand love. It just wasn't him she felt it for. It wasn't anyone but the Shadow. Her mate. She smiled at him and he didn't fight her when she curled her hand into a fist, using her ability to pull the air from his lungs.

"She's a fool, Midnight. I love you. I love you, my grathita. *Don't leave me alone. I need you."*

He never took his gaze from his mother, his vision blurred then cleared when the tears he'd never shed fell down his cheeks. She was smiling. She was enjoying being this close so she could watch him die.

"I love you. Marcus. Midnight. Stay."

His fist clenched at his side, hesitating even as his vision was going dark. How many nights had he rocked himself to sleep, wishing he was in his mother's arms? How many times had he planned a daring rescue from whatever hellhole his father had sent her to? He would be her hero. But those were childhood dreams.

His hands came up, so large around her small, dainty head and crushed her skull. The wind died down abruptly, the funnel disappearing. Midnight broke her neck, holding her close while he wrenched her heart from her chest, ensuring she would never harm anyone again. He knew he was still crying. He wasn't sure he would ever be able to stop.

"I'm close, Midnight. My love, I'm so sorry. So sorry."

But it wasn't over yet. Most of the Shadow had been slain or were retreating. But Midnight didn't care. Let them go. He wanted to end Yvan and his grand vision. He saw him there, staring at his mate's dead body as though he couldn't believe it was her. For a moment he looked so lost that Midnight knew he'd loved her too. He'd truly cared for Miriam. Then he saw Midnight and he turned to run, leaving her body behind.

"Coward." Midnight wanted to run after him, but he was too weak. Blood loss, lack of oxygen and his mother's betrayal made him stumble. Kit and Lux appeared beside him, helping him remain on his feet. He looked up in time to see Regina, her golden eyes gone black, staring at Yvan's retreating back.

The Shadow stopped grabbing his head and turning in shock to see the Reader focusing on him. For a moment it looked like he would attack her, his lips curling back in a threatening snarl. Then his gaze landed once more on Miriam's body. His hands dropped and he fell to his knees, a silent scream on his lips as the Reader destroyed him from the inside out.

"Lizbeth?"

"I'm here, my love."

"Remind me never to make your Gypsy mad at me."

"I'll protect you, Midnight. I'll protect you."

Chapter Eleven

Liz snuck out to watch the sunrise. Slathered with sunscreen and protective shades, she studied the people of the sleepy little town as they started their day. A dog barked excitedly until a woman with two children clinging to her skirts threw him a piece of bacon. A shop owner unlocked his door, stretching and smiling at the arriving day. To them this had just been another week, full of bills and dates and homework. They had no idea that a supernatural battle had taken place at the edge of town only a few days before. Only this time, instead of werewolves versus vampires, it was good versus Shadow. It was surreal, walking amongst humans. And wonderful.

All the memories of her old life were dark and full of hardship, but this morning she found herself recalling her own morning rituals. Her favorite younger brother's smile of thanks as she handed him the shirt she'd patched up for him. Blushing when she asked how it'd been torn in the first place.

To Malcolm, who hadn't had those recollections, it must have seemed like an alternate universe. Had he ever wished to be different? To be human the way she'd wished to be like him?

She turned back toward Haven, knowing she'd done this to say goodbye. Her heart would always have a place for Malcolm, he'd been so good for her. And he'd loved her. But the part of her that had been filled with guilt, the part that had been trying to prove herself worthy of her deceased husband, was finally at peace.

Midnight. He'd been recovering for the last few days. Quiet. But she knew he was still tormented. He'd been through so much. To finally regain his memory, only to learn everything he'd thought he knew about his life had been a lie. His father wasn't responsible for the secret society of Shadow Wolves and Truebloods bent on creating chaos from within. And his mother. His mother was far from the sainted victim he'd always imagined her.

She didn't know what else she could do.

The ivory box.

"What?" Liz looked down the narrow alley she'd just passed. No one was there. She could have sworn she heard…no, she was just talking to herself again. With Malcolm's voice. She needed to get back to Midnight.

She ran lightly up the stairs, shaking her head at the unmistakable sounds of pleasure coming from the other apartment. Jasyn and Hannah were still at it. They'd barely come up for air since they'd returned.

Zander and Regina had taken the children to the ruins for some family time. Alexei had come out of his trance knowing Nicolette was gone. He still hadn't spoken, poor child, but Regina said he wasn't blocking her anymore. He just needed time. Before they left, the Mediator had told Liz that the clans were in agreement. After they'd given everyone some time to recover from the shock, the Clan Trust would convene and sign the new treaty. The Nocturne Treaty. Named for Nicolette. She would have liked that.

Max was still missing, though Kit seemed sure he was alive. He could be right. He had married into the right family to know. She hoped so. Dealing with Nicolette's death had been more than she could handle.

Wyley had gone back to Dydarren land with Lux and his family until it was time for the treaty signing. He'd told her life was so exciting in Europe that he might stay for a while longer. She'd sent him with a letter for the Devas, telling them she'd come to them soon, and promising that they would always be taken care of. Just because she was Trueblood now didn't mean she would forget where she came from.

A long, loud moan echoed through the hallway, and she sighed. She had to admit, she was jealous. She needed her mate.

The door opened, and he grabbed her from behind. Pressing her against the wall. "I woke up, and you were gone." Her clothes disappeared, and she gasped at his thick erection prodding her hip. "I've spent the last hour listening to those damn Weres fucking and wishing I was inside you."

She moaned when he slid his hand between her and the wall, cupping the mound of her swiftly heating pussy. "You knew where I was. All you had to do was ask." She would have come running, she wanted him so badly.

But he wasn't listening. "I think you need to be punished, wildcat. Go kneel on the bed for your mate."

Liz shivered. This was what she wanted, her wild man, her aggressive lover. She bit the inside of her cheek to hide her smile. "Telling me what to do again?"

The hand on her sex tightened, and he growled. "Bed. Now." She obeyed, crawling up onto the bed slowly, catlike, looking over her shoulder to see what he'd do next.

His indigo eyes were dark with need. "Spread your legs wider, *grathita*. I want to see what belongs to me."

She breathed in deeply, her knees separating until she felt the cool air brushing against her sensitive clit. She knew he could see how wet she was already, how hot he was making her. Knew he could scent her arousal filling the room. But he didn't move.

Her lashes fluttered, hair falling over her arm as she watched his large hand stroking the cock she wanted in her mouth, in her ass, everywhere. Why was he making her wait? "Midnight…"

"I know, wildcat. I know what you need." He stalked toward her, the jaguar in him shining through, playing with her the way he had when they first met. "I'm not playing, Lizbeth. I'm deciding."

"Deciding?"

"Where I want to take you first. How I want to make you come. Lower your arms, that's right, present that sweet ass to your mate." She laid her hot cheek against the cover, panting now as he knelt on the bed behind her, still stroking himself, still not giving her what she needed.

Her hand reached between her legs, needing the pressure, but Midnight wasn't about to let that happen. In fact, she had a feeling it was exactly what he was waiting for. "Bad girl. I seem to remember promising to tie you up. Do you need to be tied up, wildcat? Do you need me to tie you to the bed and take you any way I want?"

"Aye. Yes. I need it." She ignored her warrior's pique and embraced the part of her that needed to be controlled. Dominated by her mate. He touched her at last, flipping her onto her back and up to the top of the bed, where scarves were already dangling from the headboard. Two scarves on each side. She sent him a questioning glance.

Midnight's wicked smile made her heart pound. He tied her hands above her head without a word, tugging to ensure they were strong enough. And then he reached back, his fingers wrapping around her ankles. "What are you doing?"

"Now, now. You said you needed it. You wanted it. Wanted me to tie you up so I can lick and fuck and take any part of you I wish, anyway I choose. Are you saying I can't?"

Great Mother. Was he really going to...? Yes. Yes he was. Her knees bent toward her shoulders and she watched wide-eyed as he tied her ankles beside her wrists, leaving her wide open to his gaze. Completely vulnerable to his touch.

"You're so beautiful like this." He ran his fingers over the lips of her pussy, sliding through the liquid heat of her, making her whimper. "I don't know how I lasted a day without tasting your honey." He bent his head to press an open mouthed kiss against her clit.

Her hips were high in the air, making it nearly impossible for her to thrust closer to his mouth, his fingers that were caressing the entrance of her sex, slipping in and out lightly. Too lightly.

"More."

"Yes, my fiery wildcat. Tell me what you want."

She licked her lips, rocking against her bonds, needing more, needing him now. "It's been too long. I can't take the teasing. I need more. I need you to fuck me."

He straightened above her, rubbing his cock against the cheeks of her ass, her thighs. "You want my cock? " He wiggled the head of his erection against her swollen clit.

"Aye. I want it. I crave it. Please."

She saw his eyes close and his body shuddered beside her. He wanted to torture her, wanted to play, but the need for his mate was too strong. All he could think of was getting inside her, deep as he could go.

"Aye, Midnight. Punish me later. Right now I need you to

fuck me, deep as you can go. Over and over and over again." He leaned in one hand gripping the headboard while the other guided his hard cock to her pussy. He had to curve his body over hers to get inside, her tied legs angling her hips until they were parallel with the ceiling.

"I've missed this. Goddess, Lizbeth. *Fuck.*"

He was shafting her. The position sending his cock so deep inside her she couldn't hold back. With every hard jackhammer thrust, she cried out his name. "That's right, wildcat. Scream for me. Tell me how much you love my cock inside you. Only mine, mate. No one else's."

"I love your big cock. Fuck me harder. *Aye.* Don't stop. Only you, Midnight. Only you. Love you. Oh Goddess, *Yes!*" She loved it. Loved the feeling of being taken. Of being totally out of control. Loved her mate touching her again, seeing her.

"I'm sorry, *grathita.* So selfish. I've been so selfish."

"Never. No my love."

"I love you. *Yes*, Lizbeth. Take it all. Baby, I'm in you *so deep.*"

Their moans filled the room, and he banged the headboard against the wall with the strength of his thrusts. Harder and faster until Liz was wondering if a person could die from pleasure.

She watched her mate above her. His fangs were bared, the tendons in his neck straining. She watched the blood pulsing through his veins, and her mouth watered. She needed to bite him. She needed to feel that sinful liquid pouring down her throat as he came.

"Fuck, wildcat." His muttered growl vibrated against her neck as he sunk his teeth into her flesh. She bit his shoulder and came at the first, exquisite taste of his blood. Her pussy tightened around his shaft as he too found his climax.

"Aye. So good. So bloody good."

"Mine. Tell me you're mine."

"You know I am. I belong to you. I've always belonged to you."

His thrusts slowed, each nourishing the other as their bodies continued to pulse with aftershocks. To Liz it felt like she could finally breathe again. Like everything was going to be fine. Better than fine. Perfect.

They licked each other's bite marks slowly, languidly. Midnight untied her and curled her against his cooling body, unwilling to separate from her long enough to cover them with the blanket.

Ivory box.

Midnight heard. He tensed against her. He didn't ask her why she was hearing his brother's voice in her head, but she cursed the intrusion just the same. "That's the second time this morning that I've heard it."

"I know."

"Did you carve that ivory jewelry box?" She lifted up onto her elbow to study his closed expression. There had to be a reason it was on her mind. She knew it.

"Most of it. The last time I worked on it, it wasn't finished."

Cursing herself for spoiling the mood, she knew she wouldn't be able to let it go. She had to follow her instincts. She dragged herself out of his arms and crawled off the large bed. Her legs were quivering, her body still tingling. She wanted him again. Already. She was turning into a nymphomaniac.

"That's a hobby I could get behind." Liz chuckled at his muttered reply. She went into the closet to pull out her knapsack, carrying it back to the bed. She sat Indian style as she dug through the contents, smiling as her hand curved around the fragile box.

"Do you know when I saw this for the first time it was right before I came to find Jasyn. And you. I couldn't stop looking at it. I had to take it with me, keep it close. I never knew why."

Midnight sat up, holding his hand out for Liz to hand it over to him. His full lips quirked, and she studied his face. The scar was gone. In a way she missed it. It had been a part of him for so long. Her wild man.

His raised brow was the only indication he was following her thoughts. "I spent a lot of time hiding in the tunnels and my room. I had an image to maintain, but it was exhausting to keep that kind of wastrel schedule. When I was supposed to be involved in some blood servant orgy, or causing general mayhem, I'd be curled up on my bed carving this box." He shrugged. "It helped me think."

"The snakes?"

"They were the secrets, the traitors in our midst, swarming around the Trueblood foundation. I'd carved out the top but I didn't add these other designs. Malcolm must have finished it for me. The moon is easy enough. Malcolm was a devout follower of the Mother."

Liz nodded. "And the thistle is a Scottish flower. That's why I thought it was meant for me."

"Maybe it was. Not sure what this design is...though it looks like...Lizbeth, do you still have Malcolm's dagger?"

She reached back into the knapsack and pulled it out. "Always. Mal made me promise to always keep it with me. Although why I'd need a dagger...what are you doing?"

She watched as Midnight studied the dagger. He started to smile, rubbing one of the raised designs just so, causing an oddly shaped pick to pop out from the hilt. "He was always the clever one." He stuck the pick into the strange, unexplained design in the corner and jiggled.

The box clicked. It had been a trick lock. No wonder she couldn't open it. "Why would he finish your box and then make the key to it so hidden?"

"Only one way to find out."

Liz wasn't sure she wanted to know. Another secret Malcolm didn't tell her. What if he was in league with the *asura*? There were some things she just didn't want to know. She looked. "It's a letter."

Midnight paled. "Read it."

She unfolded the crinkly brown parchment, looking at the top of the first page. "It's for you. But if he thought you were dead..." Midnight stood and looked in the mirror. "Read it, Lizbeth."

"My Dearest Brother,

There is not a day that goes by that I don't think of you, don't wonder where you are, or look for you in each new face I see. Sometimes I walk through the village in the morning, wondering if you are hiding around the corner, ready to sneak up on me and laugh, telling me this was one of your more elaborate practical jokes. I miss those jokes.

I do not believe you are dead as they claim, not anymore. After the war, things didn't add up. Father isn't the same man he was when we were children, and he's raising Sebastian to be a weak-minded dandy. But it's more than that. This house has eyes. And I, taking a lesson from my older brother (two minutes older, but you never let me forget it), kept my eyes open. And I found something.

But before I tell you what it is, I also wanted to let you know I am married. I knew from the moment I saw her that Elizabeth was special. That she deserved everything I could give her and more. She had such a hard life for one so young, so I took her into my heart.

She is not my *grathita*, though I won't lie and say the knowledge doesn't pain me. Yet when we could not share Unity it hit me like a message from the Goddess herself. Elizabeth is yours. I know in my heart that it is true. There is a fire in her that matches yours. And your same streak of stubbornness that always charmed me. I love her all the more for it, because she is a piece of my beloved brother's heart. I promise to keep her safe for you, Marcus. And teach her all she needs to know to survive if anyone should find out that I am continuing your good works.

I knew you were deceiving me. You're my twin, Marcus. We are connected. When I discovered your suspicions, I did some digging of my own. On the next page you'll find a list of all the current members of *asura saMsaki*. I couldn't believe they really existed, but you were right all along.

I miss you. More with every day that passes. I cannot speak your name, nor tell Elizabeth about you, for fear I will unman myself and weep like a babe. You were always the strong one. Always the one that hid our secrets. The Midnight Fog. But this one secret I'll keep for you until you return.

Malcolm"

Liz wiped the tears from her eyes. He knew. He'd always known. She looked up to find Midnight on his knees, his head bowed over in grief. But it was a healing grief. His brother hadn't given up on him. Hadn't believed he was dead. And he'd found the list of names that would protect his people. But it wasn't his secret to tell. In his mind, that honor belonged to Midnight.

She dropped the letter and went to embrace her mate. With the list Malcolm had found, Zander would be able to clean house. To make sure the demon coalition was punished and disbanded.

And Midnight knew he'd been loved. They'd both been loved. By a true hero, no matter what he thought of himself. Midnight caught and held her gaze. "I was angry at him for leaving me to rot, for loving you, for not seeing the truth. Was I right about anything?"

"We've both been foolish, my love. But for the first time in a long time, the past is past. And the future is looking bright."

He pulled her into his arms. "As long as you're by my side, wildcat."

She smiled at him, wiggling in his lap suggestively. "Not even Elvis could drag me away."

"I warned you about mentioning other men."

"Yes you did. I obviously haven't learned my lesson. I may need to retake the class."

About the Author

Stolen away by a free-spirited Gypsy as a child (though she still swears she's my mother), I spent my childhood roaming the countryside, meeting fascinating characters and having amazing adventures. As the perpetual "new kid", my friends more often than not were found between the pages of a book…and in my own imagination. I read everything I could get my hands on. At the age of 11, I read my first romance and I've been hooked ever since.

I've been a nurse, a lead vocalist in several bands, a published lyricist and even a returning university student majoring in Anthropology and Mythology. Throughout all of my varied careers, I would sigh as I read one fantasy-filled story after another saying, "Someday I want to write one of those," until one day my husband said, "So do it." And I did. Now I can't imagine doing anything else.

To learn more about R. G. Alexander please visit www.rgalexander.com. Send an email to R. G. Alexander at r.g.alexander@hotmail.com.

Kidnapping and bondage are no way to win a girl. Well, actually...

Gone with the Monster
© 2009 Lila Dubois
Book Three of the Monsters in Hollywood series.

Runako has good reason to distrust humans. His sister's murder taught him it's safer to keep his Monster form under wraps. Now comes word that a woman is making a movie that will supposedly "help" his people. He's not sure about that, but one thing is sure...Margo is too beautiful to be ignored.

Presented with the opportunity to use his people's Captive Caves—a secluded mountain fortress designed to hold hapless, tasty humans prisoner—Runako knows exactly whom he wants to star in his ultimate fantasy.

Margo knows exactly what she wants and how to get it. At least where her career is concerned. Runako is just the kind of bad boy with whom she'd like to heat up her nights. In a land of skinny blondes, though, a hottie like him would never notice her lush, Latin curves.

No one is more surprised when she finds out his version of "wooing" includes kidnapping. Forced to stand before him in chains, her paper-thin confidence is burning up fast in the heat of his desire. And when it turns out she can identify his sister's murderers, they both must decide where their loyalties lie...

Warning: This title contains light bondage, spanking, anal play, sex with a Monster and misuse of home décor.

Available now in ebook and print from Samhain Publishing.

Enjoy the following excerpt from Gone with the Monster...

Margo woke with an aching head, stuffy nose and sore throat. She scrubbed her hands over her face and groaned. She was coming down with a cold, or was she massively hung over. Last night was a bit fuzzy. She remembered leaving the office late and then...nothing.

She must have gone over to Cali's and tied one on, making this a hangover. In desperate want of aspirin Margo sat up. Chain clanked.

Wait, what?

Margo cautiously opened one eye. Rather than her tastefully decorated bedroom in the cute little guesthouse she called home, Margo was looking at stone walls.

"This is bad."

Margo stared down at the heavy metal cuff around her left ankle. It took a minute to process. Margo touched the cuff. Yep, it was there.

"Oh *hell* no."

Margo looked around. The cave had curving walls, a slightly uneven floor, and huge metal oil-filled bowls from which fire flared.

She looked at the cuff again. The memory of a massive shape, darker than shadows, filled her mind.

"Runako," she whispered.

"Yes?"

He came around a corner, appearing from the hidden inner depths of the cave. A million sharp comments died on her lips. All she could think was...*yum.*

Runako was dressed in a pair of dark grey slacks and a white button-down shirt. The shirt was open, the tails dangling and the gap showed off his truly incredible pecs and six-pack abs. The shirt looked startlingly white against his dark skin. His short hair was tight to his head, revealing the perfect curve of his skull.

"How do you feel?" he asked, walking across the cave towards her. His stride was unhurried, more of a stalk than a walk.

"You kidnapped me."

"I did."

"You can't do that."

Runako raised one brow, James Bond style. "I just did."

"Point taken." Margo crossed her arms. "I thought you were trying to fit in with the humans? Humans don't usually kidnap each other."

"Luke, Michael and Henry want to fit in."

"What do you want?"

"I want to be safe. I want my people to be safe." Runako looked away, his fingers curling into fists. Margo's heart lurched in sympathy. "I'll deal with the humans. Whatever happens."

Well that sounded ominous. Margo, who had felt mostly annoyed and not truly afraid, started to worry. Of all the Monsters she knew—a whopping total of four—Runako was the most dangerous.

"And kidnapping me means what?"

"You...you're just for pleasure." Runako rested his hip on the stone slab where she sat. He reached for her, and Margo slapped his hand away.

"I'm not some blow-up doll." Her fear disappeared under a swell of righteous anger. "And you're out of your fucking mind if you think I'm going to sleep with you."

"Who said sleep?"

"I'm not going to have sex with you."

"Why not? You want me. I can tell." Runako looked directly at her, all of his attention focused on her. It was as if she were the most intriguing person in the world.

Margo looked away so she wouldn't fall under the spell of his eyes. She looked down at her ankle and her ire flared. "You're a...a..."

"Monster?"

Margo narrowed her eyes at him. "No, you're not a monster. Monsters are delightful, thoughtful creatures. You're a jerk. A bully."

"You are truly angry," he said, leaning back in surprise.

"You think?"

"But you want me, I know it. I can feel it." He reached for her again, and this time when she tried to knock his hand away he caught her wrist.

"I want lots of things, doesn't mean I always get them," Margo said.

"You should, you deserve the things you want." He lifted her captive hand to his lips and kissed it.

Margo's heart (traitor!) fluttered. "You...you. I. Um. Oh fuck it."

Margo grabbed Runako's head and kissed him.

GREAT CHEAP FUN

Discover eBooks!

THE FASTEST WAY TO GET THE HOTTEST NAMES

Get your favorite authors on your favorite reader, long before they're out in print! Ebooks from Samhain go wherever you go, and work with whatever you carry—Palm, PDF, Mobi, and more.

WWW.SAMHAINPUBLISHING.COM

CPSIA information can be obtained at www.ICGtesting.com
Printed in the USA
LVOW062138220712

291112LV00002B/39/P